AF610546

First published in 2014 by Aloejimmy Publishing

Second Edition

A CIP catalogue record for this book is available from the British Library

ISBN 978-0-9926276-0-7

Aloejimmy Publishing

www.aloejimmy.com

Front cover: The Kon-Tiki boys (Bristol scouts) come cruising down the Thames. Aug 13, 1953.

Davie Collins and the Sundance Gang

Volume I

The Great Kon-Tiki Challenge

James Marsh

Preface

It was a brilliant sunny afternoon in the village of Surlington in Hampshire, where I was born and grew up. My wife Felicity and I had taken over the Dog and Duck Public House. As landlord, I was standing in our public bar, looking out at the high street through the clear glass window that had been fitted after the village had been flooded in the early fifties.

The same river that had overflowed its banks that day was now running peacefully on its normal course, as it went straight through and separated Surlington from our neighbours in the village of Brimly. From where I was standing I could see beyond the new bridge to where the river turned sharply after passing right the way around beautiful Banter Wood.

At the point of this turn is a clearing where an old birdhide, still in use today by the boy's gang as their headquarters, can be found. My wife and I, who met here in 1951, in Miss Plumpton's dance class, had taken over this pub from my mum and dad. They both still live here in the cottage once owned and lived in by the formidable Bumstead sisters.

Just past our pub before you reach All Saints Church, there is a small bridge over a wide stream. We have always called this the river, but it is simply a deep canal that runs off the main river and rejoins further down. From the window I could see this bridge and had the thrill of seeing my eight year old son David greeting his best friend Elliot Collins, my best friend Davies son. Davie was the village blacksmith who had taken over the Smithy from his dad in the same way I had taken over the pub from mine.

In our childhood it was me waiting and him running to meet me. We were in the Sundance Gang, he as leader and me as second in command. I thought back to the other members of that great gang and saw them all in my mind's eye as they ran up to join Davie and me. As David and Elliot chatted together the other members of my son's gang joined them, and they all rushed across the bridge into Banter Wood.

I stood still looking towards the peaceful scene of the village pond. Today the water was calm, but with a smile I thought back again to those wonderful days of the Sundance Gang and in particular to that time when we were all just ten years old. Seven of us were up to our waists in that pond and being sucked down by the mud that lurks at the bottom. It was yet another catastrophe that Davie had led us into, and boy did we suffer for it afterwards.

Chapter 1

There were eight of us in our gang. Most of us were together, slowly sinking into a large pond that our leader Davie Collins assured us could be quite safely waded.

He was as usual only partly right. The water was shallow, but the mud beneath it certainly wasn't. The result was that seven of us were now up to our waists in water and gradually going deeper as we sank further in. The air was turning blue as we cursed Davie for this latest disaster, especially as it was now looking like we would have to call for help. This was against the rules of the Sundance Gang, our policy being that we got ourselves into this mess, now we have to get ourselves out.

Quite how we would have got out of this particularly nasty situation I don't know. Fortunately for us Paul Edwards was not as adventurous or as easily led. He had not followed us into the pond, so was able to rush back to our little village of Surlington, on the south coast of England, to raise the alarm. Davie had got us into so many bad situations that most of our parents were resigned to it. But this caused an even bigger stir than usual, not only did it involve them but we needed the local fire brigade to free us from the clinging mud that by now had us very much in its clutches.

A ladder was swung out over the pond, so they could crawl along it and attach a rope to us. One by one we were pulled out onto dry land. What a sight we now presented, soaking wet from the waist down, with our legs covered in thick oozy mud.

My father lost no time in taking me by the ear and leading me, screaming with the pain and humiliation of it, back to our home, which was the village pub, the Dog and Duck.

The back yard was full of barrels and crates of empty bottles that were due to be picked up later that day by the brewers dray when it called with this week's delivery for the pub. Here I suffered the indignity of having to stand still while my father hosed down my lower body to get the awful smelly mud off my clothes and legs. Only when it was all gone was I allowed to go indoors and up to the bathroom, where I had to put my clothes into the basket for washing, then run a bath before I dared to come downstairs for my tea.

My mother was more sympathetic to my predicament than my father had been. She had some cheese sandwiches and an orange squash ready for me, as well as four of her wonderful homemade pickled onions. As I sat at the kitchen table devouring this she looked at me.

"It's Davie Collins again isn't it?"

When I nodded she shook her head saying, "it always is."

Davie Collins and I had been best mates since we started at the village school just over five years ago. Since then we had been in one scrape after another. The trouble was that Davie had the most brilliant ideas that always seemed so exciting and easy to do. But then inevitably, snags appeared and it was always too late for us to do anything about it.

My mother understood this, but worried that I would be injured or worse during one or another of these madcap schemes and would warn me of dangers that could come my way. She was a lovely woman, tall and slender and I loved her as much as any boy could love his mum. She didn't crowd me or stand in my way, but was always on hand whenever she was needed. As long as she knew where I was going each day, she tended to leave me to myself.

My father however was a very strict disciplinarian. I had to be very wary whenever things went wrong because his punishment was swift and hard, but fair. I always knew why I was being punished and vowed each time not to do that particular thing again. He ran our pub in the same way gaining the respect and liking of all our customers. They were mostly village people who preferred to use the Dog and Duck, than the other pub at the far end of the High Street. This one, the White Swan, was used mostly by visitors to the area.

My name is Billy Taylor and I had been born in this lovely village nestling by the side of the River Gest in Hampshire. Surrounding us was our playground, Banter Wood and we always had a wonderful view of this from the bedroom window of Johnnie White. His father ran the flour mill, and from here we could see for miles across the countryside around us.

This village, recovering from the war that had ended some five years before, now in 1951 was almost back to pre-war days. We had not suffered anywhere near as much as the large towns and cities in Hampshire, places like Southampton and Portsmouth to name just two. Only two bombs had actually fallen on us, these being jettisoned by German Bombers on their way back home. One of them hit the village hall and did quite a lot of damage, but luckily it was at night so the building was empty and no-one was hurt. The other landed in open country and just ripped up a few trees. Because we were relatively safe we had a lot of children evacuated here for their own safety from the big cities.

I was born in 1940 so when hostilities ceased I was nearly five years old and really beginning to take notice. I started at our little village school in late 1945. This was run by Miss Tuttle, whose job was now a lot easier than it had been in recent years with all the extra children to teach. She was strict, but a lot of fun as well.

From the first day at this school, Surlington Village Juniors, I met the boy who was to become my best friend. He was the son of our blacksmith and his father was a man in great demand. Many of the farms around us had horses, as did many of the delivery rounds men. All of them needed shoeing and were brought to Mr. Collins to have this done. Davie and I sat next to each other in a class of twenty five children. Fourteen of these were boys and the rest were girls. It wasn't long of course before we all knew each other very well and eight of us had formed our own gang. We called it the Sundance Gang because we had heard from Mickie Tranter, who was a cowboy nut, about a famous outlaw called the Sundance Kid. Davie liked the sound of that straight away so our gang was named after this man.

Davie had natural leadership qualities and inevitably became the gang leader, and I as his best friend was second in command. This grand title simply hid the fact that it was me who had to implement whatever ideas he came up with. Surlington was like so many other country villages and had one main street, where all the shops and businesses were to be found. With the school and church being opposite each other in the centre of the High Street, this place became the centre of our lives as well.

All week we went to and from school, and on Sundays were in the choir of the church, looking like little angels as we sang our hearts out at both the morning and evening services.

Miss Tuttle the school mistress we had to be careful of. Like so many of her contemporaries she seemed to be fitted with radar and always knew what we were doing. I never managed to work out how she did this. For instance, Davie or one of the others would smuggle a note to me under the desks, but before I could read it she would bark out, "Billy Taylor bring that note out to me."

Then I would have to read it aloud to the whole class. How did she know the note had been passed? She was always facing the blackboard, but it happened on so many occasions. Davie gloomily said we might just as well shout out our gang business to everyone because they will all find out anyway when the notes are read out.

Miss Tuttle was the one who caused us the most embarrassment over this problem because most of our lessons were taken by her. The rest of the staff came in on a temporary basis. These were Mr. Bond, who had lived in the village for a great number of years. He seemed, at forty six, very old indeed to us and we often wondered why he wasn't already in a home. He took us for woodwork and we had to be careful here as well. One day Mickie Tranter had made a mess of a simple dovetail joint. As soon as Mr. Bond saw this he called us all round Mickie's bench and pointed out his mistake, so we knew where he had gone wrong. It was humiliating to him and we tried that little bit harder to make sure this never happened to us. So despite Mr. Bond being so past it, we did learn a lot from him.

Miss Trout came in twice a week and took the girls for needlework and sports. She may have had a funny name but she was a lovely lady and caused feelings in most of us boys that we didn't fully understand. The girls all thought we were daft. There was also Mr. Gardener who took the boys for sports and PT.

We had regular gang meetings in our secret hideout, a converted hide that was once used by bird spotters but was now very definitely ours. It was situated at the top end of the wood, in a clearing near where the River Gest turned sharply to the left to flow on down between our village and the neighbouring one of Brimly. Above the door was the biggest rule of the gang displayed in a notice outside which said '*No Girls Allowed*'

Davie and I would sit on our slightly raised orange boxes, while the rest sat on theirs watching us. The boxes having been acquired from the green grocery shop run by Keith Andrew's dad.

Sitting here I looked, as I had done so many times now, at the members of the Sundance Gang. We were a fairly well balanced lot and got on really well together. Davie was by far the most dominant member, he was well built and this wasn't at all surprising as his dad was massive. This of course helped him enormously in the heavy work a blacksmith is called on to do. Davie was so much like his dad in many respects.

We then had Mickie Tranter, whose parents were the village grocers. He was small in stature but not in nature. He made up for his size in the daring way he tackled everything he was challenged to do, and he usually did it with a cheeky grin on his face. Sometimes he was wayward and didn't always listen to warnings, so ended up in very embarrassing situations indeed.

Sitting next to Mickie was fishmonger's son Phil Landers. He was the tallest in the gang and had a full head of flaming red hair. But he became very angry if any of us called him either red or ginger. His hair may have been that colour but he liked to be called by his proper name, so it was simply Phil. In all other respects he was a very likeable lad. Always willing to join in, but the drawback he had was looking most awkward in the short trousers we all had to wear. Because he was so tall they made him look ridiculous.

Paul Edwards, the son of the postmaster, was a mixture of adventurer and cautious Joe. Sometimes rushing thoughtlessly into things while at others drawing back and pointing out the flaws he could see in whatever we were doing. He lived above the little post office that visitors always admired and used their brownie box cameras to photograph. It may have been small but it did all we needed.

Johnnie White was particularly popular because he was the son of the local miller. His family lived in a big cottage beside Turvy Mill, one of the very few windmills still in use for grinding flour. To have an excuse to be in and around a windmill on a daily basis was sheer heaven for us all. Johnnie himself was a fairly easily led boy, only holding back when challenged to do one crazy thing after another. His trouble was, always believing us when we assured him that what we wanted to do was quite safe. His parents often had a go at us when he came home in tatters or wet through. He found out much too late that our assurances were quite worthless.

The mill fascinated all of us and we spent so much time getting in the way of Mr. White and his assistant. They put up with us because they could see we were genuinely interested in the production of the flour that went into so many shops in Hampshire. It wasn't just the grinding of the flour that held out attention either, but also the wonderful shire horses that pulled the hay carts, full of wheat from the surrounding farms. We always managed to have treats for them in the form of carrots, bread or sugar lumps, courtesy of Mickie Tranters mum and dad.

Keith Andrews was a happy go-lucky lad who usually did his share in the dare games. He, like the rest of us, would end up time after time in the water. It didn't do to not like this if you wanted to be in our gang.

Lastly we had Danny Meadows, who even at this young age was consumed with his interest in the Royal Navy. His father was the manager of the only bank for miles around, but his grandad was a famous naval Admiral. He wanted to follow his grandad into the Navy and perhaps someday rise to that rank himself.

Top of today's agenda was the problem of getting a note past Miss Tuttle, and Paul Edward's soppy feelings for one of the girls in our class, Angela Ford. There were ten girls altogether and we got on reasonably well together. In the playground we sometimes divided up if the boys were playing football, since girls were completely useless at this men's only game. If we were just chasing, or playing other ball games then the girls usually joined us.

Romance was still a long way in the future for any of us, and sex was something we knew absolutely nothing about. So why was Paul Edwards suddenly going dopey whenever he looked at Angela Ford? He seemed to go completely weak at the knees. The whole silly situation had reached a point where he would sit at his desk and just gaze across the room at Angela, who was taking absolutely no notice of him at all. So something had to be done about it, and quick.

Looking around at the gang from his lofty perch at the front, Davie opened the meeting.

"Right you lot."

This was his normal opening gambit.

"We have two things we need to talk about today. First how to get a note past old Tuttle without her knowing about it, and then the far more important thing, helping out at Turvy Mill with the painting. So first on the agenda, how do we fox the Tuttle?"

He didn't know what the word agenda meant, but it sounded good to him so he always used it.

"How do we get a note from old soppy pants over there, and get it delivered to Angela Ford?"

Paul Edwards turned a distinct shade of red over this.

"The floor is open to suggestions."

He had heard this termination on a radio discussion show and immediately adopted it, adding it to his repertoire of sayings. There was an awkward silence following this which was eventually broken by the high, rather squeaky voice of Phil Landers.

"Couldn't one of us have a fit or something? Miss Tuttle would have to look after whoever it was, then in the confusion the note can be shoved on Angela's desk."

There was a lengthy silence. Davie always did this whether he understood what had been suggested or not, it made him look more important as he considered a plan put forward for his approval.

"Yes that could work, but who is going to have the fit? Phil, this is your idea so I think it should be you who does it."

Phil was immediately in a panic.

"Why me?" he asked, his voice even more squeaky than usual.

"I don't know how to do it, what do people do when they have a fit?"

He was met with six blank faces, all but one of us having no idea of the answer to this.

It was the studious banker's son Danny Meadows who answered.

“Well, one of my cousins has fits and I was there once when it happened. She was right as rain and playing cricket in the garden with us. She was rubbish at the game of course, but we sent her after the ball all the time. If it got hit too hard it went next door and their dog would try and chew it. The fielder had to wrestle the ball out of the wretched dog’s mouth then run back with it, wiping the dog spit off on the way. She was good at it and did it time and time again. That is until she suddenly fell on the ground and started writhing around. We didn’t know what to do and were mighty glad when her mum, my aunty Mavis, came running out. She set to work and turned Primrose, that’s my cousin, on to her side in the recovery position. Then checked her airwaves to make sure they were clear. That led to her coming out of it and returning to normal.”

“Ok,” said Davie “That’s a very good description, but what do you mean by the recovery position?”

“I don’t know, she just turned her onto her side.”

Patiently our leader looked at him. “Which side?

“Oh,” spluttered Danny, “her right I think.”

“So that’s all you have to do then?” asked Davie, now using his superior leader’s voice.

“Turn the person who is having the fit onto their right side?”

“Yeah that’s all aunty Mavis did.”

“Why?” barked Davie.

“Well how do I know?” replied a now thoroughly rattled Danny. “She just did.”

“Ok fine, but what about, what was it you said, seeing if her airwaves are clear?”

At this he just got a big shrug of the shoulders, Danny had no more idea what this actually meant than the rest of us.

"Right then we'll bypass the airwaves," said Davie. "Phil, come out here and have a fit."

Awkwardly and very nervously, he came out into the space between Davie and me and the rest of the gang and just stood there.

"What do I do?"

"Writhe," shouted Davie.

"How?" he wailed.

"Oh for Pete's sake," said our saintly leader. "Show him Danny."

Danny hesitated, then came forward and got down onto the floor to give his impression of a person having a fit. He drew his legs up under his stomach them thrust them out again, at the same time arching his back. He continued to do this for a few minutes before collapsing in an exhausted heap on the floor.

"That's as best as I can remember it," he said as he tried to brush the dirt from the floor off his clothes. He alone was very particular about this and tried to keep them clean and dry at all times. But as a member of this gang of course he had no chance of achieving that.

"Okay Phil, your turn," said Davie.

Phil got down onto the floor and in fairness to him really did try to give an impression of a fit. But he was so tall and had such long skinny legs that the whole thing looked like a caricature from a Disney cartoon, and wouldn't have fooled anyone. Let alone the redoubtable Miss Tuttle.

Things were beginning to become a bit tense, until Keith Andrews, who had been very quiet up until now, suddenly joined the debate. He had recently been to the little cinema, the only one in the village, and seen a spy film. It was one he liked a lot and it had given him an idea.

"What about a decoy?"

"What's one of them?" I answered him.

He then explained what he meant by this. In the film the good guys had to get a roll of microfilm to the British Embassy in some far off foreign country, but the bad guys were on to them and watching everything they did. So they hatched a plan to send an agent with an attaché case through a supposedly safe route to the Embassy. This case contained nothing more than one of the agent's wives grocery lists. While the foreign agents were following this decoy, another agent, unknown to the bad guys, got to the embassy and delivered the vital microfilm. This sounded simple and easy to deploy.

Our leader looked across the floor at Keith, "Gentlemen we have salvation."

There followed a long discussion about how we could bring this about. A note, about a gang matter, would be dispatched along the usual route. Going under the desks of Danny, Johnnie, Paul, and finally and inevitably to me. Miss Tuttle would, of course yell at me to bring it to the front of the class and read it aloud.

While I was doing this, and holding the attention of the whole class, the note to Angela Ford would find its way onto her desk by the same route. This was a foolproof plan all we needed now was for poor soppy Paul Edwards to write the thing for us.

With this decided we could move onto the second item on today's agenda, the painting of Turvy Mill. This was done once every ten years and kept the beautiful old mill looking resplendent. It was all white, and on sunny days you could see the blue reflection of the water from the nearby river Gest. When the sails were turning it was like something from wonderland, and we were all very proud that we lived in an area that still had a working windmill.

The miller knew each and every one of us, because of our friendship with his son, so Davie had volunteered all of us to help with this task. It would be good practice for us learning to paint something as large as a windmill, and would also earn us some much needed pocket money.

The only thing Davie hadn't done was to ask us if wanted to do it, our co-operation being taken entirely for granted. Of course we all said yes. The fact that we would be earning something for this task had been pounced on by our treasurer Danny Meadows. He kept an old biscuit tin in his bedroom at home in which he kept all of the gang's money. Not quite as safe as the vault at his dad's bank, but it did the job. Our current balance was one shilling and four pence (roughly six pence). So we certainly needed funds.

Davie explained that the painting would be done by means of a cradle. A wooden platform, with ropes attached to pulleys at both ends would be lowered slowly down the side of the mill. We would paint the building using brilliant whitewash. Quite a simple undertaking it seemed. As usual though, we didn't give anywhere near as much thought to this venture as was needed.

I could think of one problem straight away, two of the gang had trouble when we went tree climbing. They were alright when there were lots of branches, but if the trunks went straight up with only limited footholds, then neither of them could tackle these. Turvy Mill was very high indeed, but Davie dismissed it as not important.

"We'll all be up there together so we can see they're both alright."

The price agreed with Mr White, who unknown to us had already talked the whole thing over with our parents before agreeing to let us help, was an enormous two shillings each. Multiplying this by eight, it came to the king's ransom of sixteen shillings.

Once this was realised there was not one dissenting voice, especially when we were promised a cream tea after the job was finally finished. We would paint the whole of the outside of the building, with Mr White and his assistant, whose name was Trevor. Once this was done the grownups would be left to do the much more difficult job of painting the four huge sails that turned in the wind and operated all of the machinery inside the mill.

So the scene was now set, the note caper would take place with immediate effect during the next week. Painting at the mill was arranged for the first week of the summer holidays in just three weeks time. Two ventures had been well planned and nothing could possibly go wrong.

Three days later Paul Edwards finally made up his mind what to put in his note to Angela Ford. He would not show this to anyone, not even Davie. We all loathed the afternoon arithmetic lesson, so any distraction here was welcome. The first note was sent on its way, the usual journey under the desk to me. Typically just as I took it from Davie, old Tuttle did it again.

"Billy Taylor, bring that note out here."

So I walked out to the front and had the usual job of reading aloud to the rest of the class what were our private matters, in this case an emergency meeting in the woods after school to discuss an important matter.

"The Sundance Gang will meet at our hideout after school today to discuss the state of our finances and what we need to do to put this right."

As I read this I was watching note number two making its way to the desk of Angela Ford. I knew Miss Tuttle was watching me as she always did. This was working just as we wanted and was a triumph for the Sundance Gang. The note duly arrived in front of a very startled Angela.

Then the impossible happened, as I came to the end of our note she looked straight across to a certain desk and said the words that sent shivers of doom through all of us.

"And now Angela, perhaps you will be good enough to share the contents of the note that you have just received."

We were all in a state of shock, how on earth could she know? She was watching me, how could she have seen the other note? I looked quickly across at Paul, and he had gone a peculiar shade of white.

Angela slowly stood up, looked at the note and wailed, "Please Miss I can't read this out."

"Never-the-less that's just what you will do," and the way she said it left no room for doubt.

With her cheeks flaming red Angela read out Paul's love letter. Although the term love letter was perhaps not quite a very good description.

"Dear Angela," it read. "I love you, do you love me? If so, answer yes."

"Well," Miss Tuttle said. "That's very interesting isn't it? And what is your answer?"

Angela glared across the room at poor squirming Paul and shouted as loudly as she could, the single word "No."

Poor Paul, I have never before or since, seen anyone go from white to bright red as he did then. His love had been thrown back in his face, and in front of the whole class, most of who were now convulsed in laughter. He wanted the ground to open and swallow him up, and we were all so sorry for him. Even Miss Tuttle now looked on him with pity. He may have liked Angela, but a note like that, oh no.

Through playtime that day and for most of the rest of that term Paul was the butt of so many cruel jokes. His only salvation being the loyalty we all showed him. Davie got into at least three fights defending him. All of which he won because he was good with his fists, much to our credit on a lot of occasions.

At our next meeting in the hide we were discussing how this disaster had happened. The whole thing was re-enacted two or three times, so that we were convinced we had done nothing wrong. The operation had gone as planned until Miss Tuttle ruined it with devastating effect.

How she had accomplished this none of us had the least idea. I was out at the front of the class reading the decoy note aloud and she was watching me. How then could she possibly have detected the second note? No-one had any answer to put forward that could explain this.

The only good thing to come out of this whole sorry mess was that Paul was very definitely over his silly crush on Angela Ford. He loudly declared that for as long as he lived, which of course would be for at least another hundred years, he would have nothing more to do with girls. In this we all heartily agreed.

We all thought that Paul needed something to cheer him up after such an ordeal. So it was decided to take sixpence out of our club kitty, leaving the princely sum of ten pence in the biscuit tin, and buy him a quarter of the new toffees that had just come into the grocery store where Mickie Tranter lived.

Sixpence was a lot to spend on just a quarter of sweets, not to mention we would have to part with two sweet coupons for them as well. But a club member was in trouble and we were going to cheer him up.

The toffees were brought back to the hide, where they were ceremoniously handed to Paul. They were meant as a special treat for him, but he of course handed them round so we all got two toffees each. The Angela problem was then put very firmly behind us.

We now had two things to take into consideration, besides the major undertaking of painting Turvy Mill. These were the battles fought annually against our arch rivals, the boys of Brimly village school. We played a football match at the end of the summer term and then a game of cricket at the beginning of the autumn one.

Brimly was a small village on the other side of the River Gest and was nowhere near as good as Surlington. Our village rivalled theirs in so many ways.

We had two pubs, they only had one. We had a blacksmith, they didn't, and we had Turvy Mill. This was a huge thorn in their side as it was the only one of its kind in this part of the country. We also had a small fish and chip shop that served the best chips in the country, they had a small van that came round once a week, and the chips were nowhere near as good as ours. Because of this the boys of that village did everything they could to undermine us.

We had to be careful when we were out, to make sure they were not anywhere around, laying traps for us. They would also try to pinch our apple scrumping pitches from the surrounding farms. We had a lot of orchards on our side of the river which were a boy's scrumping paradise. They tried on so many occasions to muscle in on this.

The two legitimate functions had been contested between the schools for more years than even our parents could remember, a very long time indeed. Coming up first was football. It was our schools turn to host this event and it was to take place on the green behind the duck pond in the centre of the village. This was a very large grassed area, and was a natural football pitch.

All of the Sundance Gang were in the Surlington team, as well as three others. One of these, a boy scout, was not a member of any gang but was a natural at sports. So even though he was not one of us, he came from our village and went to our school. Therefore he was very much a member of not only our football team but, and this was much more important, our cricket team as well. On the last day of the summer term, just before the start of the wonderful six weeks summer holiday, the two teams faced one another. To say there was no love lost between us was putting it mildly, we loathed each other.

Miss Tuttle gave her usual speech about sportsmanship and may the best team win, and all that nonsense. But all we wanted was for the game to start so we could get at them. A blast on the whistle brought ten boys on one side and ten on the other swarming all over each other. In fairness the ball was kicked a lot, but so were we. A tackle coming in was aimed, not at the ball, but at the legs of the nearest member of the opposing team. And we were as bad as one another at it.

When Mr Bond wasn't looking, and how anyone as old as that could keep up with us and referee a football match was another thing beyond our comprehension, we would commit outrageous fouls. Tackles from behind, deliberate trips, and fouls on the goalkeepers were carried out by both teams.

Davie had already avenged the bad kicking he had received from Frank Thornton, the Brimly captain, in last year's fixture, by letting fly with a huge punch to this boy's midriff. Somehow we reached half time, with seven of ours and six of theirs, needing first aid. The score was nil-nil. Now well into the second half, with the whole school roaring us on, even the voice of Miss Tuttle yelling "Come on Surlington," I suddenly got the sort of chance I had always dreamed about.

Many times in the small yard behind our pub, I had been playing soccer for England. The team was always desperate for a goal but unable to score it. That is until the marvellous, unstoppable Billy Taylor found the ball at his feet. Swerving this way and that he took off, shrugging off the tackles of the opposing team, until he let fly from just outside the penalty area, and saw the ball fly into the net for the winning England goal.

Now here, in this important game for us, the scene was suddenly unfolding before me. A pass from the Brimly team had been intercepted by Phil Landers and he punted the ball downfield to me. I was midway in the Brimly half of the field so without any sign of hesitation took off. It was happening just as I had imagined it so many times. The ball was glued to my foot and I was running with it, at the same time evading the desperate tackles flying in from Brimly. I ran past them then rounded their goalkeeper who had come out to the edge of his penalty area to try and stop me. I was having none of it and simply punted the ball wide of his outstretched hands.

Then I jumped over him, regained the ball and with no-one near me drew back my right foot and let fly with a mighty kick, sending the ball towards the now empty net. As it flew through the air, I could imagine the delight and praise from everyone in our team. Not just them, but the whole school and the village. I would be the hero, the scorer of the brilliant goal that sent our arch rivals home in defeat.

I stood with my breast swelling, as that ball travelled through the air in a perfectly straight line that would take it right into the centre of their goal. I wasn't even alarmed when it suddenly started to veer to the right, it would still go into the net. But the veer got worse and worse, until with the groans of everyone now ringing in my ears, it flew well wide of the far post and ended up nearly hitting the corner flag.

I of course was devastated, and even more so ten minutes later when this scene was re-enacted. This time the boy with the ball was the boy-scout whose name was Martin Izzard. He did everything with it as I had done, but finished it off properly, and the huge din as it went into the Brimly net was deafening. The end result was Surlington 1 Brimly 0.

Martin was mobbed and carried shoulder high from the pitch at the end of the game and I, with dragging feet trailed in last. Davie, as all best friends do, lingered and waited for me to reach him. Then putting his arm around my shoulder said "don't worry about what happened it was a darn good try, and anyway it was the wind that carried the ball away from the net."

That's why we were best friends and fellow Sundance gang members. Davie, taking the trouble to tell me that, cheered me up straight away. And the victory tea in our village hall certainly helped as well. We were one up on Brimly and now had to do it all over again in six weeks time when we took them on at cricket. We now had the long summer holiday in front of us. The first thing that had to be tackled was the painting of Turvy Mill, and that didn't go according to plan either

Chapter 2

A great deal of effort would be needed for us to play our part in smartening up Turvy Mill. As I sat at the breakfast table that morning eating my usual bowl of corn flakes, my mother was pacing around the kitchen. This was the way she always acted when she was agitated about anything.

"I know what will happen," she was saying. "With Davie Collins and the rest of that bunch around you things always go wrong, and you will be up high when you start painting. I'm worried you will fall off and hurt yourself, or even worse."

This outburst was not usual with my mum and just showed how worried she was.

"But mum," I said. "Mr. White will be in charge and he won't let anything happen to us. We'll be on a cradle that is firmly fixed by ropes. We'll be okay."

"Yes, and you'll all be painting using buckets of whitewash, what sort of state you will end up in can only be imagined. Do you know how much clothes cost these days?" she challenged. "You may think money grows on trees, but it doesn't. It has to be earned, so I expect you to look after the clothes we buy for you."

So now with these words still ringing in my ears, I set off to meet up with the others.

Mickie Tranter lived closest to me so I called for him first. An ordeal for me as his youngest sister was starting to act peculiar whenever I was around. She would come running to the door and say hello, usually offering to share her sweets, or whatever she had at the time. When I asked Mickie why she did this he just shrugged and said, “She’s a girl.” I decided the best thing to do was avoid her as much as I could, but this proved to be easier said than done.

The rest of the gang were waiting for us by the bridge over the river, just past the church, and together we made our way to Turvy Mill. Mr. White and Trevor were already there and before we did anything we were all given aprons, made from flour sacks that we would have to wear over our clothes to keep them clean. This suited me after the lecture I had been given, and the rest of the lads had experienced similar from their mother’s as well.

Aprons may look sissy, but if they do the job and keep us clean then so be it, besides there was no-one around to see so it would be alright. Once these had been put on and everyone had stopped laughing at each other, Mr. White started to explain what we would have to do.

“Okay boys the first thing we have to do is to clean nearly ten years of grime off of the building. So for the next two to three days that’s what we will be doing. Trevor and I will be at each end of the cradle and we’ll operate the pulleys to either higher or lower it. You will all sit in a line between us. Take your time at first, don’t just go straight in and try to gain a world speed record for whoever can do the job the fastest. This is not a race. You will have to get used to the way the cradle moves. If anyone is scared or gets into any kind of trouble, yell out at once and we will come and help. Just use the scrubbing brushes with firm even strokes. That way we can get most of the dirt off before the first coat of new whitewash goes on. Alright boys any questions before we start?”

There were none so we went to the cradle and prepared to be lifted aloft. All of us wondered just what we had got ourselves into. We were only ten years old, and with the exception of Phil Landers not very tall. So as we looked up at the top of Turvy Mill it seemed to reach right up to the sky.

Before I could change my mind and pull out, which was certainly what I wanted to do as I looked at the height of the building, there was a creak of ropes going through a pulley. Suddenly the wooden cradle hit my backside. From there my feet left the ground and with the others I started the lift to the top.

As we went higher my stomach went lower. Panic was not far away, and the other two who had no head for heights were just sitting with their eyes firmly closed. But, incredibly, the gang spirit prevailed again. Davie threw one arm around me and stretched the other out to them, then started singing. It was a song we had to sing often at school, the great British favourite Greensleaves. He was using the rather rude words we had made up ourselves for this song and soon he had us all joining in and actually laughing.

When the cradle reached the top of the building I gazed around at the familiar countryside I knew so well, but had never seen from such a vantage point as this. It was like sitting at the top of the big wheel when the fair came at Easter. Gone was the fear and in its place wonder. Also I could see into the mill from the small platform at the top of the tower. I had never been this high before and had always, until now, looked up at this place.

There were two levels, the upper and lower bin floors. We were just above the upper floor, at the same height as the machinery that turned the upper shaft. Although now standing idle, it was usually turned by ratchets that were operated by the sails. The bin floor was below this, and from here grain was poured from a position immediately above the three great turning stones where it was crushed into flour. After which it falls into chutes on the meal floor before being collected into sacks for delivery.

I could only state these facts because I have a very good memory. Mr. White had explained it all to us on quite a few occasions now, but I and the rest, with the exception of Johnnie White, still never really understood the whole operation.

But we were now outside and after we had got used to the swaying movement of the cradle work did get under way. We had a bucket of soapy water and a scrubbing brush and now began the hard work of using these tools to remove as much grime as we could.

Two of us, Danny Meadows and Phil Landers were not much use. These were the two who really didn't like heights so they were using their brushes with one hand only, the other one holding on for dear life to the cradle. We did manage to remove a lot of the dirt on that first day and got half way down the tower before Mr. White called a halt.

One thing was very apparent as we got off the cradle and dropped the last few feet to the ground. Without the aprons we would have been very wet and dirty by now. All day we had been splashing soapy water against the side of the mill and it went everywhere. Yes it did the job, but went over us as well. Of course there were accidents when a full brush of soapy water landed right in someone's face or their laps. When this happened retribution was swift and the perpetrator had the same thing done to him.

Mr. White kept a very keen eye on this behaviour and when it threatened to get out of hand, stepped in to put a stop to it. He knew the value of what we were doing however. While we were having a go at each other we were forgetting to be scared and the job was being done well as a result. Once we took off the filthy wet aprons we were surprisingly clean and dry underneath and able to go home and present ourselves to our parents and gain their approval.

It took us three days to wash down both sides of the mill. On each side we stopped when we reached a point just about four feet from the ground. From here we could easily jump the rest of the way down onto solid ground. At the front of the mill, this stopping off point was just above the small door that led to the inside. The bottom part, as well as the huge sails would be painted by the grownups, and we didn't envy them that.

For the next four days we had the time of our lives as we applied the whitewash that Mr. White had mixed for us, onto the sides of Turvy Mill. We worked from buckets, wielding the brushes like true painters and decorators, with all the excess whitewash going onto our aprons, and little if any landing on us.

So, amazingly, just over seven days from the time we were first lifted aloft, most of Turvy Mill now gleamed in the summer sunshine and really did look splendid.

Mr. White had jumped from the cradle on this, the last time we would use it, and he and Trevor had gone inside to get our promised cream tea ready for us. Before this he had shown both Davie Collins and his son Johnnie, how to secure the pulley ropes on both sides. Then all of us discarded our sack cloth aprons for the last time, and eagerly claimed not only our large wages, but also that wonderful cream tea. It was smashing and all of us made sure that not one crumb was left.

Feeling happy, well fed and decidedly wealthy we came out of the mill to start back to the village and our various homes. As we walked out into the sunshine each one of us instinctively looked up to admire once more the wonderful job we had just completed.

As we did this there was a definite creaking noise which rapidly grew louder. Then before our horrified eyes the cradle, which should have been firmly tied into position gave a lurch and slipped to one side. Johnnie White had not secured the pulley rope properly and the combined weight of the eight buckets that were still on there made the rope on that side slip through. Suddenly nothing was holding it on one side and the result was horrendous.

The cradle collapsed altogether and eight buckets containing varying amounts of whitewash were airborne. We watched in horror as they turned gracefully in the air then emptied their contents in one great white torrent.

Glued to the spot and totally unable to move we were completely engulfed in this whitewash waterfall. All of the care we had taken in the past few days to keep ourselves clean and out of trouble had gone out of the window in less time that it takes to blink. One moment we were clean and respectable, the next we were not only soaking wet through but white all over as well.

Johnnie White disappeared into his house by the side of the mill as his mother arrived, and what a time she gave him. We could still hear her shouting as we dragged our way home knowing the same sort of reception awaited us.

I was whisked straight upstairs by my mother. She ran a bath, telling me to stand in that one spot and not to move until I was told to. I wouldn't have dared to disobey her in the mood she was in at that moment. When the bath was ready she made me get in, clothes and all, and there I stayed until she had scrubbed all of the white wash from me using the hard Sunlight soap she used for all of the family washing. She rubbed this into my hair, all over my arms and legs, and all over my clothes as well.

I was in that bath for well over an hour and in between gasps as she applied the soap had to listen to her down crying Davie Collins. This was unfair as none of what had happened today was his fault but he was blamed anyway.

“It’s always the same, you go off from here clean and tidy and come home looking like a tramp or worse, and this?” she spluttered as she rubbed harder and harder with the soap. “Oh words fail me.”

My father thankfully was away for the day on business for the pub. Otherwise I shudder to think what I would have had to face from him. All of the others had similar experiences and in poor Johnnie White’s case he had to help his dad clear up the mess our accident had made outside the mill.

It was a horrible end to a great seven days. To make matters worse the story went round the village and soon of course everyone knew about our downfall. We had to put up with sniggers from all of the village girls whenever we were out. The boys, not only from Surlington, but far worse from Brimly, sang at us. As we went on our way we could hear the Vera Lynn song made famous in the war.

This was sung with one word given emphasis and sung much louder than the rest of the verse. We had to put up with repeated versions of “There’ll be blue birds over the ‘White’ cliffs of Dover.” But when two weeks later, the redecoration of Turvy Mill was complete we all looked at it with pride. Despite what happened at the end, we had done our part in making this grand old mill look so good again and we saw this as a triumph for the Sundance Gang.

Now though, just three days after the great white wash disaster we were all once again in our hideout in Banter Wood. Davie looked at us in his usual way before opening the meeting. Firstly there was praise for the way we had worked on the mill, leaving out all reference to the end result, before starting on the next Sundance Gang agenda.

"Boys," he announced, "we are going to build a raft."

There was a general stir of interest in this and little Mickie Tranter replied straight away

"That's great Davie, how do we do it?"

"Do you all know about the Kon Tiki expedition?" Davie asked.

There was a big nod of approval because we had indeed heard of it. A raft built in 1947 by a Norwegian man had been sailed across the Pacific Ocean. It was the sort of thing boys of our age could only dream about. We had talked about this before because it had been covered in school, but not in any great detail. Yes it was a master feat for anyone to accomplish, but we were always taught that British was best. And as this was a Norwegian expedition it was not considered important enough to dwell on with any real efficiency.

Davie told us that a film had been made about it and it was now showing at our little cinema, the Roxy, which we all simply knew as the flea pit. The film about the Kon Tiki was a documentary of the actual building of the raft and the voyage itself. The man behind the whole thing and the leader of the expedition was called Thor Heyerdahl.

When the raft was completed, he and five others set sail on their epic quest that took them 4.300 miles across the great Pacific Ocean. The raft was made with balsa wood from Peru.

We had heard of this wood, but never actually seen any. All we knew about it was that it was very light yet strong.

At the first opportunity we resolved to call in on Mr. Bond at his little bungalow to see how much information he could give us about this wood, and where we could get some. It must be good stuff because the Kon Tiki took 101 days before they smashed into a reef on a funny sounding Island. It was such an achievement that the documentary about it won an academy award at this year's award ceremony in America. They may have taken 101 days to cross the Pacific Ocean, but we planned to take just one day to travel two miles down the River Gest to the little harbour, where cargo ships from Europe unloaded their wares.

Here we would have to be careful, because on a little slipway a large sailing ship was moored. She was a three master and they looked enormous reaching up into the sky. This was a training ship for Royal Navy Cadets where they had to learn not only seamanship but small boat handling. Every day teams of these cadets were out in rowing boats doing all sorts of manoeuvres. What they would do if their way was to be blocked by eight boys on a homemade raft we shuddered to think. The Petty Officers in charge were big men who shouted a lot, and we didn't want their anger to be directed at us.

Now back at headquarters the first plans were initiated. I think that's the right word, Danny Meadows' dad used this word a lot when things had to be done properly in the bank. The task was simply how to make our version of the Kon Tiki. They had used nine balsa wood tree trunks, each 45 feet long. These were lashed together with hemp rope, and also lashed to the two cross pieces of 18 foot long balsa wood logs. The cabin they built for the crew to live in was made of bamboo, as was the enormous mast. Steering was done with a large oar at the rear of the raft.

First then how do we get the balsa wood for our own Kon Tiki?

Mr Bond was in his garden tending his prize roses. He had won best of show for the past three years for these at our annual village show. To say he was surprised to see us was putting it mildly. We didn't particularly like seeing him at school, so to drop in on him at home, in the holidays, was unheard of. When he heard the reason for our visit however, he invited us indoors and listened patiently to our plans for our raft. This would be equal to the Kon Tiki, providing we could get the materials we needed.

After Davie had outlined our most urgent need he looked around at all of us.

"This is a good idea boys, I don't see why you can't build a very sturdy raft, certainly one that will carry you on the journey down the Gest as you have described. But balsa wood is not easy to get hold of. It's a specialist wood, used by modellers mostly in this country. And it's expensive because it has to be imported."

Seeing our blank looks he explained this, "that is, brought into the country. To get the amount you are talking about would cost a fortune and would take you at least twenty years to save up for. And even if you could get the money it would be difficult for any wholesaler to get in such quantity. No, your best bet is to use wood that is easy to get your hands on. I know you have a hideout in Banter Wood, and I also know that in 1943 a German bomber jettisoned two bombs as they flew over here. One hit the town hall."

We all nodded at this as we knew about the war damage to this old building that had now been restored. The clock that still worked perfectly had been reinstalled in its original place.

"The other," continued Mr Bond, "landed in Banter Wood. It uprooted a lot of trees so there will be enough wood there for your needs."

We were excited to hear this and should have realised it ourselves. Mr. Bond now revealed that there was more to him than any of us had thought. Before we made our way home, he took the trouble to draw a blueprint for us on how to properly construct a raft using tree trunks.

So the first problem was solved, where to find the wood necessary for the main part of the raft, the bit we would all be sitting on. Now we had to plan the mast and what we would use as a sail. The mast we decided could be made from one or other of the small branches lying around on the ground all over Banter Wood. We could pick one that was thick and long and could be tied into position without much trouble.

The sail would have to be made. Paul's mother, Mrs. Edwards at the post office was nominated because she actually owned a sewing machine. We just neglected to tell her that we had given her the job. Her acceptance and indeed eagerness to help us being taken entirely for granted.

So on a bright Wednesday morning in the third week of our holidays the Kon Tiki expedition got underway. We had been scouring the woods for some time now and had come to the part of it where the German bomb had fallen and exploded.

Mr. Bond had been right about this, there was now a clearing that hadn't been there before the war with Germany began in 1939. This was because all of the trees that once stood proud were now lying all over the ground. We started looking among these and picked out nine stout tree trunks, all averaging 12ft in length. The problem we had now was how to get them all back to our hide out where the raft construction was to take place.

Davie, of course, had thought of this and now came up with the solution. We had been told at school, by the lovely Miss Trout, in one of the few lessons where she took all of our class about the lumberjacks of Canada. These men not only chopped down trees but then tipped the trunks of these into the swift flowing rivers that carried them downstream to the various sawmills. In order to ensure they got there without jamming up and causing a big logjam across the entire width of the river, these men jumped onto them and rode them all the way downstream, jumping from one to another to keep them going straight.

We had the mighty, well fairly big anyway, River Gest at our disposal. So, at the word of command from our leader the first tree trunk was tipped into the river and held by the bank while it was decided who would be the first to leap aboard and ride it down stream. Davie did it fairly and asked for a volunteer, but we all drew back and silence was the only answer he got.

The tree trunk didn't look at all safe. It was rolling round and round as the rivers current swept by it and I for one couldn't see how anyone could even get onto it, let alone stay on. Davie, faced with this silence now nominated his choice of who should have the honour of being the first Surlington lumberjack.

Inevitably, his gaze found and fastened onto little Mickie Tranter.

"What you looking at me for?" he wailed, "I ain't doing it."

"Mickie," said Davie, "it's easy, all you have to do is jump on that tree trunk, then as the current carries it downstream, just keep your balance. Keep the trunk near the bank and grab hold of something solid when you come to our camp, and that will stop the trunk from going any further."

"Jump on it?" replied Mickie. "The blooming things moving around all over the place, I'll fall off."

"Of course you won't," countered Davie "your weight will stop it moving around so the rest will be easy."

It still took a lot of persuasion to get Mickie to agree to do it. He had said when we started out he didn't want to get too near the water today because he had some of his better play clothes on and didn't want to get them wet.

We helped him onto the tree trunk and once he was standing, roughly in the centre of it, we all let go. The result was calamitous. One minute Mickie was standing there, and then it rolled over so swiftly that all we saw of him were his shoes as they disappeared under the water, and the huge splash he made.

Davies first thought was to save the tree trunk as it was starting to move off on its own. Paul Edwards and Danny Meadows caught hold of it and held on, while the rest of us helped the now soaking wet Mickie Tranter out of the water. He stood on the bank, the clothes he wanted to keep dry now so wet they were clinging to his body. But instead of anger, this happy go lucky boy now looked at us all and said with a laugh.

"Well that's me sorted. I can't get any wetter can I? So, who's next?"

Good question and the answer was all of us. The only way we could transport these tree trunks was for all of us to be in the water and hand guide them downstream. Davie again assured us that if we kept close to the bank, the water was so shallow it would only be our shoes and socks that would get wet.

Wrong, we slipped and slithered our way down the Gest, all of us at one time or another falling over in our attempts to keep our respective tree trunks on course. And when, amazingly, we all arrived at our campsite and grounded our trees, all of us were soaking wet. But it was mission accomplished and as it was a really hot day we went swimming in the river while our clothes dried.

So now we had the tree trunks for the raft base, a stout branch for our mast, and several old shirts that would be fashioned into a sail. Paul Edward's mother had been less than pleased when her son told her of our nomination for her to make our sail.

"Do you think I've nothing better to do?" she shouted at him. "What with the post office to run and all of the housework as well, it's all I can do to keep up with the mending I have to do for you and your father. And you're no help, always coming home with your clothes in tatters. Last week alone I had to repair two pairs of your trousers, how you managed to rip the seat out of them I can't think."

Paul had slunk off after this. The episode with the trousers coming about from one of our climbing games. This was when Banter Wood became Sherwood Forest and we were all merry men to Davie Collin's Robin Hood. Four of us at a time being up in the trees, ready to drop down on the other four as they made their way through the Forest.

Twice when Paul did this, he managed to catch his pants on the branches. But to say he ripped the seat out of them was a gross exaggeration. All that happened was that the seam gave way at the back and had to be sown together again. But mothers always make such a fuss about things like that. So it looked like we would have to make our own sail.

First of all we had to put together the main raft. The Kon Tiki had been roped together using stout hemp rope and ours would be equally fastened, using the clothes line we had borrowed from the garden of Mrs Featherstone. Well she didn't use it very much so she wouldn't really miss it would she?

Our nine tree trunks were all laid out together, and we were now trying to get the rope from the clothes line underneath. We had two shorter pieces going across underneath and the rope had to go around that, as well as around the whole of the raft.

Davie had borrowed a small axe from his father's smithy and used it to cut V-shaped pieces out of each of the tree trunks, front and back. The rope nestled into these and held the whole thing together nicely. Our mast was fixed in the middle, Davie again using the axe to cut a round hole for this to fit into, then it was roped to the underside of the raft. We had more orange boxes that were used to make a cabin on deck for us to sit in as we made our epic journey down the Gest. Lastly, but just as importantly, we fixed another much thinner tree trunk to the rear of the craft, this would be used as our steering wheel.

Phil, Paul, Johnnie and Keith were then told to take off their shirts and hand them over.

"Why?" they all shouted.

"For the sail of course," Davie told them. "We need at least four shirts to make it big enough for what we will need."

"Ok, but why us?" asked Phil. "If I go home without my shirt my mum will kill me."

"So will mine," the others all shouted in unison.

"You won't lose them," said Davie. "This raft is going to last us a long time and we only need the sail when we are going against the current. At all other times we will use paddles. Each time you will all get your shirts back, simple."

That word had been used by Davie on so many occasions before and I personally couldn't remember a time when after saying it, disaster didn't follow.

Amazingly though, it seemed to pacify the others and they dutifully removed their shirts and handed them over. This was just to see if four shirts would be enough, and after holding them up against the mast and being satisfied with the result, the four shirts were returned to their owners.

The first voyage of the Surlington Kon Tiki raft took place the next day. We needed all of our combined strength to launch it from the bank where it had proudly sat overnight into the waters of the River Gest. We were just going to try it out before embarking on our downriver trek and Davie nominated first two, then four and finally all of us together to stand on the raft to test it for sea worthiness.

Mickie Tranter had made a fuss again, not surprising really because he was one of the first two to get on the now floating raft. "Me again," he shouted as he was pushed onto it, then Keith Andrews after him. They were followed by Danny Meadows and Phil Landers. When, with four boys standing on it, the raft was still floating and in one piece, the rest of us joined the crew.

Oh what a thrill that first trip was, just from one side of the river and back. But it was on a raft we had built ourselves and soon we would be going on a longer and much more exciting trip. So the plans were made for the Kon Tiki expedition, Surlington version, to take place in three days time. This was to give us time to harass our mothers for sandwiches and drinks to last at least one day. And anything else we could lay our hands on.

As I lived in a pub, it was thought I would be able to get some bottles of brown ale, but the others had not reckoned with my dad. He knew the stock like the back of his hand and if he caught me trying to sneak off with some of it my feet wouldn't have left the ground. Punishment would have been swift and hard. If there was one thing my parents had drummed into me it was never to steal. And taking drinks from the Dog and Duck would certainly be viewed as theft. Sneaking off with a clothes line, that would eventually be brought back anyway was not stealing, merely borrowing.

The same could be said for our scrumping grounds, the apple orchards that abounded on our side of the river. Scrumping, or to give it its real name, stealing apples, has been a British boys pastime for centuries. All fruit farmers allowed for some of their stock to disappear into the pockets of local boys every year. We were experts at it, and our favourites were big bramley cooking apples that grew in large quantities in an orchard by the banks of the Gest, and only a matter of a mile or so from our camp.

We now had to plan this year's scrumping and to deal with the problems we encountered last year. Bramley apples were just right for picking in early September. We were now in late August and they were already weighing down the branches of the trees. This was the time we usually devoted to filling our camp with these delicious apples.

Bramleys are cookers but are sweet enough to be eaten as well. So we always made sure we had enough for ourselves to eat, and also to take home for our mother's to make the dreamiest apple pies anyone could wish for. We always told them the apples we had were simply fallers that we had been allowed to pick up.

If true this would have been allowed, but scrumping was much more fun. The Bramley apple orchards had high fences around them. Too high for us to climb, we had been given another idea by Paul Andrew's dog when we watched it tunnelling under his back garden fence to get out. Brilliant we thought. We can do exactly the same.

We dug under the high fence, and four of us squeezed our small bodies through this to get into the orchard. The apples we picked were thrown over the fence into the river where, downstream, the other four were all in their bathers in the water. They collected all of the apples floating down towards them and brought them into our hideout to be divided up between us all.

Last year though we suffered a horrendous defeat at the hands of our arch rivals, the boys of Brimly village. They had watched us in our first successful year, but when we tried it again they had beaten us at our own game. Losing to them at anything really rankled with us but to lose our precious apples as well was totally unacceptable. They had done it by having their own boys in the river just beyond the bend where our boys were as usual waiting for the apple bounty to come floating towards them. Most of the Bramleys that we threw into the water were simply being plucked out again, by them. We were left with only the few that got by.

When we had realized what was happening and charged to intercept, they all ran off waving our apples in the air for us to see. It was the laughter that got to us and right there and then we had vowed that this would not be allowed to happen again.

So we now planned the operation, *No Bramleys For The Brimlys.* This was written on a large piece of cardboard and was hanging up inside our headquarters. So we were ready, both for the Kon Tiki expedition and revenge on the boys from Brimly.

Chapter 3

The next few days were so eventful that the raft voyage had to be put off for a while. To start with we had to protect our scrumping grounds from a raiding party of Brimly boys. Davie had gathered us all in the Bramley apple orchard. This, as well as several others growing various brands of British apples, was owned and run by Farmer Bentley of Maybrook Farm. It was mostly arable, but there were dairy cows as well as sheep and pigs.

We knew the Brimly boys would try last year's trick again. They didn't have a great deal of imagination, and something that had worked once was good enough to try again. We knew also that they would be watching us to see when we started scrumping so we had gone in earlier than usual to pick up some of the fallers that were still lying about in the grass. These were left there on purpose. Once they had turned rotten they went straight into the large bins to be turned into fertilizer and sprayed on the fields in autumn. Six of us gathered as many of these rotten apples as we could, while the other two made sure our enemies weren't in sight. We carried them to a point just above the bend in the River Gest and there piled them up.

We then openly went back to Maybrook Farm. Four of us, as usual, scrambled under the fence. The other four, instead of being in the water were standing by the piles of apples. True to form the Brimly boys came sneaking out of the bushes on their side of the river and started to get changed into their bathers. Before they could complete this, however they were engulfed in a huge wave of rotten, smelly apples being thrown with gusto by Mickie Tranter, Paul Edwards, Phil Landers and Keith Andrews. These four were very good at throwing. They had strong arms and their aim was good.

The result saw the Brimly Gang, in various stages of undress, and covered with rotten apples, running as fast as their legs would carry them back to the safety of their village. What their reception was when their mother's saw them we could only guess. But we hoped they would suffer punishment as a result.

As for us we now carried on as usual. The four apple throwers went further downstream before changing into their bathers and gathering up all of the delicious Bramley Apples that floated down to them as we threw this bounty into the water. The plan now was to take all of these into our headquarters and divide them up between us, but only seven of us were present. Phil Landers had disappeared. No-one had seen him go off so we didn't have any idea where he was. He came back some thirty minutes later, and was labouring under the weight of the largest apple any of us had ever seen.

He came into the hide and thankfully dumped this on the floor. Once we had all got over the shock of this Davie found his voice.

"Where the hell did you get that?"

"It was growing on a tree in one of the gardens of the cottages over the way. As soon as I saw it I couldn't resist it."

"But you know we don't scrump from gardens," said Davie.

Phil countered by telling us the tree where he had taken this apple from was laden down with more. The owner couldn't possibly know he was missing one because of the amount that was still there.

The discussion about this raged on for some time. Davie was very particular about gang rules and scrumping apples from private gardens was definitely in the 'against' column. The main reason being that small garden growers were far more likely to notice if their apples started disappearing and were always on the watch at this time of year to make sure this didn't happen to them. Quite how Phil Landers had managed to scrump this monster without being noticed baffled us all.

"How did you get it here without anyone seeing?" I asked.

"I stuck it up my jumper," Phil said. "When Mrs Pallisar asked me what I had there as I passed her house, I said it was a bag of sandwiches. She just said 'that's nice dear' and went indoors. It was easy."

We couldn't really argue with that. So now we had to decide what to do with the biggest apple any of us had ever seen before. To divide it up between us was certainly the most popular suggestion put forward.

But Davie said "No boys I don't think that's the best thing to do. Just look at it, what a great apple pie that will make."

We looked at it, and in our minds eye could see this enormous pie, oozing with apple and having large helpings put onto plates in front of us, covered with creamy custard. That was enough to convince us. We just had to nominate which of our mums would make the pie but went home that evening with this issue not settled. According to all of us, each of our mothers was better than anyone else at apple pie making. So without agreement having been reached the giant apple remained in our hideout.

It was early the next afternoon when we met up again. Most of us had to do various jobs at home all morning, in my case helping my dad move the empty barrels ready for the dray men when they called just after lunch. We walked as usual through the village on our way to Banter Wood, but suddenly stopped dead in our tracks. On one of the lamp posts in front of us was a notice.

WANTED

The Prize Apple grown by Col. Worthington-Pugh has been stolen from the tree in his garden. It was to be exhibited in this year's Surlington show and has been nurtured by the Colonel over the past months. The apple, the biggest of its kind ever grown, has been removed from the Colonels garden by vandals. A reward is offered for its safe return.

As we stared at this notice a loud rasping voice that we all recognised at once, rang out behind us.

"And I suppose you lot don't know anything about this do you?"

Constable Herbert Thackery, who patrolled not only Surlington village but two others in the district as well, Brimly and the much smaller Larwood a few miles up the coast, now stood glaring at us. The theft of the apple had been reported to him by the Colonel.

Eight boys standing together in front of him suddenly became little angels. Halos appeared above our heads and in our best choir boy manner we all said "No Constable Thackery, this is the first we have heard of it."

"Really? Now why do I find that hard to believe?"

Davie now alarmed us as he stood up to this law enforcement officer.

"We have our own rules about good behaviour officer," he calmly said. "We don't steal apples or anything else."

"That's very good to hear," the constable retorted. "I won't have to use my gloves on you then will I?"

This was a chilling warning. There were two things that could and certainly would happen to us if we were caught stealing. First our parents would be informed, which would bring swift and decisive punishment to us all. Or, and this was just as bad, Constable Thackery would use his rolled up leather gloves to swipe us round the ear. This had happened to me on at least three other occasions and boy did it hurt.

We now beat a hasty retreat and got to our hideout in the woods as fast as our feet would carry us. Once inside we looked at the giant apple still in its place on the floor and couldn't believe that something like this could bring us all so much trouble, and trouble was certainly the way to describe our position now.

Every one of us knew who Colonel Worthington-Pugh was. A veteran of the Second World War, he was a short plump man with a red face and an extremely loud way of speaking. I knew this well because the Colonel spent most of his evenings in the Public Bar of my dad's pub. My bedroom was upstairs just behind this and every night I could hear people talking. Colonel Worthington-Pugh's was always the loudest voice I could hear. It echoed way above everyone else's, with one exception.

There were two sisters living in our village and they were Maud and Ada Bumstead. Miss Maud Bumstead ran the village sports club. She was a big lady and we found her frightening. It was her theory that girls should be allowed to take part in sports that were played only by men. To this end she was recruiting girls to play her favourite sport of rugby league. The men of Surlington simply thought she had a few screws loose and laughed off such a preposterous idea. Rugby, as well as soccer was played by men. Women were absolutely incapable of keeping up with the rigors of either of these sports.

Her sister Ada Bumstead was in charge of the riding stable in the village and she had at least six girl grooms helping her to run it. It was this lady who rivalled the Colonel when it came to speaking loudly. Every evening, when the horses had been settled for the night, they all came down to our pub. And every night, as she came into the bar, Miss Bumstead yelled at my dad to see that her 'Gels' as she called them, were all served with drinks. She would then start telling everyone in the bar about her day, her wonderful horses, her gels and the way they looked after them and the stable. Her voice always rose above the level of everyone else's. Davie knew most of these girls because from time to time they came to his dad to have the horses shod.

What I heard every night was a mixture of Colonel Worthington-Pugh telling all within range of him, stories of his army career. Always ending on what he at least thought, was a funny note. Then he would roar with laughter, his great voice echoing with a loud 'Haw Haw Haw'.

On the other side of the bar Miss Bumstead would be doing the same thing and at her laugh line would also laugh louder than anyone else. In her case it came out as 'Hee Hee Hee'. I heard this contest so many times and had reached the point where I simply took no notice and usually went off to sleep pretty quickly. Last night though I had listened to the Colonel shouting about what he thought of thieves, low life that could rob a man of the prize he had spent so much time and effort on. They should be publicly birched. I didn't give it much thought at the time, but now it all made sense.

My dad had to intervene. He diplomatically told the Colonel that while he understood why he was so angry, he couldn't have him shouting and issuing threats in his bar. At this the Colonel stormed off and the pub got back to normal.

I however did not. I had heard other people saying how they admired the Colonel because of the way he looked after his apple trees. Always pruning them when they needed it, and keeping them free from any sort of damaging fungus. His apples always won prizes at the annual Surlington show. So to lose his prize asset was not going down well at all.

I told the others this and we all looked at each other, no-one knowing what to say.

"We could take it back," said Phil hopefully.

"And say what?" asked Davie. "Sorry Colonel we didn't mean to pinch it? He'll kill us if we do."

"Well we've got to do something," I said. "My dad was saying all morning that this sort of thing must be stamped out, and that the Colonel was so angry. I kept saying 'yes dad' all the time, I never realised it was our fault."

"Ok," said Davie, "let's think this out properly. The Colonel was going to show this apple at Saturdays show yeah?"

We all nodded at this.

"Right then, all we need to do is to sneak it into the show tent Friday evening so it's there when the judges arrive on Saturday."

"But the Colonel will have to have it labelled so that the judges know it's his apple their looking at," said the studious Danny Meadows.

"Alright know it all," said an exasperated Davie. "So we'll somehow get it back to him on Friday so he can take it to the show himself."

He looked round at seven blank faces and then came up with a brilliant, completely foolproof plan for the return of the apple to its rightful owner.

"We're going to do our raft trip on Friday so we'll take the apple with us. When we get back it's bound to be early evening and we all know that by then the Colonel will be down at the Dog and Duck. So all we have to do is to sneak through the woods to the pony trail then follow that until we come to his back garden. We can leave the apple there for him to find when he gets home. Then we can all get home ourselves and listen to Dick Barton."

This was a radio serial that was broadcast on the wireless every night at 7.15. We were addicts of this programme, as were thousands of boys and girls around the country. Dick Barton Special Agent got into one hair raising scrape after another. Along with his side kick he managed every time to get out of it, and solve whatever case he was working on. It was routine stuff really, but we loved it so much that the woman of the village took it in turn to ring what became known as the Dick Barton bell. Each evening, at seven o'clock this rang out, resulting in us, as well as all the other boys in the area at the time, running out of the woods and into one house or another to listen to the next exciting episode.

Davies plan sounded perfect and we went home happy that night. Not only looking forward to sailing down the Gest on our now very sturdy raft, but also getting out of the difficult situation with the prize apple. My mum was waiting for me as I came into the back kitchen of the Dog and Duck and she too was upset at all of the fuss the Colonel was making over a dam apple.

"We have to work all the hours God made to keep this pub going," she said as she put my tea in front of me. "And that old blowhard has nothing better to do than grow apples in his garden and win prizes."

It was a long time since I had seen my mother as angry as this, but inside I was a happy boy because I knew we were going to solve this problem the very next day.

The next morning, after breakfast my mum was again not overjoyed at the amount of food I was asking her to make up.

"What are you going to do with all of this?" she asked. "I know you've got a big healthy appetite, but even you can't get through this much food in one day."

"But it's going to be shared between us all mum," I countered.

"Oh I see, so I have to feed the whole lot of you do I? And what are the other mother's doing to help?"

"Well Mrs Tranter is giving us drinks, and the other mum's are chipping in with food and clothes we may need. We'll be out all day,"

"Well you make sure you are all very careful today on that raft. If it was up to me you certainly wouldn't be going, it can't be safe, a raft that you and that lot built yourselves."

"It's ok mum," I answered. "We can all swim so if anything goes wrong we'll be alright. Besides dad has already been and looked at the raft and he's happy with it."

This was true. Two days before, my dad along with all the others had been to our camp site to inspect the raft. They had gone over it looking at everything, particularly the ropes and knots we had used to make sure they didn't give way once we were out on the water. When they finished I had swelled with pride when he said "This is a good job boys, we can't find a thing wrong with it. Have a great trip all of you."

As they walked away we could hear them saying that if they were still our age it would be them taking this trip instead of us. At this we were all smiles. They didn't know we had used David Callows knowledge of knots, learned in the scouts, and it was these they had been so pleased with. He was from Surlington, but not in the gang. Not yet anyway, but that was about to change.

The day of the big raft adventure got underway in glorious sunshine just an hour before lunchtime. It was difficult to convince some of our gang of this though. Most of them wanted to start on the food even before we had set off. However I was in charge of the nosh and I made my presence felt in no uncertain way.

"We will have food at 12 o'clock," I loudly announced, and would listen to no arguments on this point. Phil Landers tried to convince me that he needed food at once as he had a very rare condition that could only be put right by regular platefuls. It was very well put really, but of course not believed. He had to wait, along with the rest of us for our official lunch break. This was planned to take place at Salmon Leap, a popular picnic spot a mile downstream on the Brimly side of the river.

We loaded all of our equipment onto the raft, spare clothes, bathers, food, sweets and cigarettes. Theses had been obtained by Davie on one of his trips with his dad in the surrounding area. We had all started smoking now and got over the stage where the smoke nearly chocked us and started coughing fits. We could hold the cigarette between our fingers and inhale the smoke with ease. But buying them was a problem because we came from a small village where everyone knew us. So telling local shopkeepers they were for our parents would simply not work. Especially for me, dad ran his own pub and bought his cigarettes from his own stock. Davie had to sneak into various shops outside our village that served many of the farmers and get cigarettes for us from there.

Now with everything aboard we set off on our epic journey down our own river on our very own raft. She handled beautifully and we sailed a straight course down the middle of the Gest. I enjoyed it all so much, the movement of the raft beneath us as well as the scenery along the banks. We were followed at one stage by a family of swans and their cygnets and we were thrilled with that.

We came eventually to Salmon Leap and Davie, who was on the steering oar, guided us skilfully into the bank. Phil and Mickie jumped off and secured the ropes to the branches of the nearest trees. Now we could tuck into the wonderful food that we had brought with us, mainly prepared by my mum. We had sandwiches of cheese, ham, luncheon meat and corned beef. As well as this we had tomatoes, fruit and various fizzy drinks. We over indulged and had to spend time lying on the banks of this lovely river to recover. We lay here for half an hour, and then had a cigarette each, after which we dozed off.

It was a noise that woke us up, the sound of branches snapping in the trees beyond the picnic area. We put this down to the wildlife that roamed these banks, urban foxes, and roe deer. Now fully refreshed, we once more boarded the raft and cast off to continue our voyage. At first everything was alright with the raft handling well and steering a straight course. But suddenly, without any warning, she veered dramatically towards the bank.

Davie was on the steering oar trying desperately to correct this strange behaviour, when the whole structure began to tear apart. The ropes holding the raft together parted with a twanging sound and before we knew what was happening we fell through the now unsteady logs straight into the water. We all surfaced in time to see our wonderful raft breaking apart and floating off downstream. Worse than that, as we trod water we could see on the bank, the grinning faces of all the Brimly gang.

There were nine of them and they were all there. Frank Thornton, their leader and fierce rival of our own Davie Collins, Bill Grimes, Bob Yates, David Conner, Michael Allbright, Peter Warnley, Edie Compton, John Kingsley and Joe Lancaster. The raft had broken up and was now floating away downriver taking all of our spare clothes, sweets and fruit with it.

But far worse, bobbing in the water was Colonel Worthington-Pugh's prize apple. I soon realised why Bill Grimes was wearing only his bathers. He was the best swimmer in the Brimly gang and he dived into the river. As the Colonel's apple reached him, he grabbed it and swam back to the bank. Now the whole lot of them held it aloft and jeered at us before running off taking the prize apple with them.

We turned and swam back against the current, to our own hideout and there came out of the water and collapsed on the bank in exhaustion. The Gest wasn't the fastest flowing river in Hampshire, but it did have a pretty strong current. Swimming against this needed staying power and it didn't help that we were all fully dressed.

What a sight this was, with all of us soaked to the skin. We looked at each other in total disgust. We had lost heavily to our bitter rivals from the other side of the river. They had robbed us of our wonderful raft and all of the spare clothes we were carrying. These had been meant as replacements if anyone did accidentally fall in the river. Now they were downstream and on their way to the Solent, where the Gest eventually ran out.

Our sweets had gone as well, and when we thought of the cost of these in money and coupons we were hopping mad.

None of us had even mentioned the loss of Colonel Worthington-Pugh's prize apple, which we knew that the Brimly gang would be tucking into. There was now no way he was going to win the Surlington prize for the best apple at Saturday's show.

We couldn't go home because each one of us had convinced our parents that this venture was going to be a great success. If they saw us in this state we would all be in for it in a big way. We therefore spent the entire afternoon swimming in the river, our clothes hanging from the branches of the trees to dry. When we finally got home and told our parents of the breakup of the raft there were, as expected, a few raised voices. We agreed not to mention that the raft had been deliberately sabotaged by those devious plonkers from Brimly Village. Instead it hit an underwater obstruction that ripped the ropes apart. Despite our desperate efforts to save her the raft had torn apart and we had been forced to abandon her. No mention was made of the apple that had been snatched.

Things weren't helped in this direction by the fact that Colonel Worthington-Pugh only managed to get second place with another of his apples. In itself this wasn't too bad, or so we thought anyway. But when it was confirmed that first prize went to his next door neighbour, sparks flew in a big way. These two had no liking for one another and were very much bitter rivals.

The Colonel of course was ex-army, and didn't we all know it. Whenever he got the chance, he would go on and on for ages about his troops in the last war, and the army in general. If he managed to corner us at anytime he would tell us, "You boys should be in the army cadets, that way you'll find out what a grand institution the army is." We were always bored to tears with this because we knew by now just what we wanted to do when we grew up. Everyone supposed I would follow my parents in the licensing trade and take over the Dog and Duck when they retired. But not so, I wanted to be a railway engine driver and was already determined to achieve this goal.

The colonel's next door neighbour was a likeable man, in our opinion anyway. This was Lieutenant Commander Phillips. We liked to talk to him because his stories of the war at sea were thrilling. He had been with the British Fleet that eventually caught up with and sunk the German Battleship Bismarck. We listened to him telling us the story of the way the ship was hunted down after she sunk the pride of the British Navy HMS Hood. Danny Meadows was even more fascinated by this, and other stories of the British Navy at sea, than the rest of us and we knew the reason behind this. Danny's dad might have gone into banking, but his Grandfather was ex Royal Navy and so that was his dream when he grew up.

We had already been taken, last year as well as this, to Portsmouth's famous Naval Dockyard for Navy open day. This thrilled us all as we could go onto one warship after another, frigates, destroyers, cruisers, giant aircraft carriers and to our enormous joy, a submarine. Here we were shown round and everything was explained to us.

So we liked the Lieutenant Commander, but Colonel Worthington-Pugh positively loathed him. So to come second to him at the show when he knew his original entry, the apple that was pinched from his garden, would have given the prize to him was too big a disappointment for him to take with any sort of grace. He made such a fuss about it in the Dog and Duck that even Ada Bumstead was drowned out.

Also in the bar that night was the Reverend Frank Morley, who was trying to have a quiet drink with the church choir Mistress Mavis Trump. He tried to pacify the Colonel but did it the wrong way. Saying it was God's will that his next door neighbour won the top prize just angered the now thoroughly red faced army officer even more.

"What do you know about it Reverend?" he shouted, his voice now rising so loud that I had to cover my ears as I lay in bed upstairs. I didn't quite understand the next bit, when the Colonel accused the Reverend of coming into the pub flaunting that Trump trollop. Everything went quiet after that as my dad showed the Colonel the door.

The next morning after breakfast I told my mother I had heard most of the row in the bar last night and asked what the Colonel had meant when he called Miss Trump a trollop. We knew the lady in question because she took us all for choir practice on Tuesday and Thursday evenings.

As long as we sang in tune we were alright, but if anyone started whispering or got out of tune she would yell "Stop." Then glaring at us she would say, "Boys this is a hymn you are singing, it is a song for God himself so please do it correctly. I know you can because you have all done it before, so we will now do it again and keep doing it until we get it right." And she always kept to her word on this. Sometimes we had to do a hymn over and over again until we were falling asleep with boredom. It didn't pay to upset this lady. So what is a trollop and why had she been called this?

My mother was strangely hesitant in answering this and finally said that a trollop is what people call a lady who is as dedicated to her job as Miss Trump was. Sometimes people get jealous of this and think up unpleasant names to call them. And that the Colonel was just upset at not winning the top prize, so trollop was probably the first name he thought of. It didn't mean anything really, just that old man letting off steam. The old windbag was about to let off a lot more steam as we were going to find out to our cost. The Brimlys got a message to him that it was one of us who stole his apple and boy did the balloon go up.

Chapter 4

We met up at the hideout the next morning, having suffered huge telling offs from our mum's because of the state of our clothes when we got home. They were dry alright but creased up and decidedly smelly, and my dad exploded when he saw me. It meant I would get extra jobs to do for the next few days as punishment, so I didn't know how much time I would have to spend with the gang.

Today Davie was madder than at any time since I had known him. We all sat watching as he paced up and down in front of us, this being strictly against his normal practice of sitting on the raised orange box. Now he was shouting about what had just happened to us and the reason for it.

"We thought of everything that could go wrong and took the right precautions. We even had a change of clothes for anyone who might fall in. What we didn't think of was sabotage by that Brimly lot. And we should have done."

Nobody said anything to this we all knew he was right of course. The Brimly gang were our sworn enemies and they would do anything to discredit us, as we would to them anytime we got the chance. But we had been so busy building the raft, and making sure she was seaworthy, that we forgot all about this bunch of no hopers, in a substandard village, on the other side of the river.

The people who lived in Brimly would not have agreed with our assessment of their village. It was in fact a beautiful place, with shops that rivalled ours in quaintness. There was a grocery store larger than the one owned and run by Mickie's parents, as well as butchers, bakers, and fishmongers. They even had their own small theatre where plays and musical shows were put on every few weeks. Indeed some very famous showbiz personalities had appeared there at one time or another in their careers. But, as far as we were concerned they, along with every other place in Hampshire, were substandard when compared to our lovely village. So to have been beaten and humiliated in this fashion by a gang from over there, just wasn't acceptable in any degree and we all knew it.

"Ok," Davie said. "We have two things to do, and we haven't got much of the holiday left to do it in. First, we need to build another, even stronger raft to accomplish our downriver trip, but more importantly, we need to get even with those bloody Brimlys.'

To use language like that showed how angry our leader was. His father was a huge strong man, not one anybody with any sense would pick a fight with, and he drummed into his son the need to be honest, good mannered and polite at all times. His mum, nowhere near her husband in stature but just as tough, if not more so mentally, left Davie in no doubt what his fate would be if she ever caught him stealing, being cheeky to adults, or swearing. He made the mistake once of using language his mother didn't approve of and found her hand landing with smarting force on his backside.

This was forgotten though as we sat in our bird hide headquarters brooding on their victory, and how we could get back at them. It would have to be something spectacular that would cause them huge embarrassment, and if they got hidings for it as well then so much the better.

For the new raft we would use long logs, as before, but wouldn't rely on ropes to hold them together. We would also use four barrels, one on each corner, which would give much more stability. I, of course, was delegated to supply these.

"Where am I going to get them?" I wondered.

"Don't be daft," Davie retorted, "from your dad's pub."

All of the others had agreed with this leaving me completely outnumbered. It made perfect sense to them, beer comes in barrels so a pub would have many of these lying about and we only needed four. The problem was my dad. It was true not all the barrels went back to the brewery we always did have some in our yard. But I would need his permission to use four of them to build a second raft, and what his reaction would be when I asked him I could only imagine.

David Callow knew more about raft building than the rest of us put together. He was in the Surlington branch of the Boy Scouts which held raft races on the Gest every year. They always seemed to have a great time, even though most of them ended up swimming in the water after falling, or being pushed off, their raft. One of the things we discussed was the possibility of David joining the Sundance Gang. Not only would this make us even in numbers to the Brimly lot, we would also have David's know-how when rebuilding our raft.

Nobody could come up with a good enough scheme to get back at the Brimly's so we left with this still unsolved, but began to feel better now we were thinking of action. We reached home to a silent reception that none of us liked the look of, only when we got indoors did we found out why. My parents stood glaring at me in the kitchen, before my mother spoke first.

"We've just had a very nasty session with that old man Worthington-Pugh."

That she left off his rank showed how displeased she was, and the look on my father's face said it all.

"He has just received a letter telling him who is responsible for the theft of his giant apple, and it accuses all of you in that blasted gang of yours," my dad roared. "He's been here, and to the other boy's homes creating merry hell about the loss, not only of his apple, but the prize it would have won him. How could you do something like that, stealing from our neighbours, and bringing disgrace to all of us? Bend over that chair."

I did as I was told and he brought the large bat that mum used for beating carpets in the yard, down on my backside. When it was over I was sent straight up to my room, and there was no mention of my tea.

Later though, my bedroom door opened and dad came in carrying a tray with a plate of mum's delicious homemade cottage pie, a huge hunk of bread and a fizzy drink.

As I fell on this my dad said, "If you're going to do something like that, the first rule is don't get caught. What were you thinking of? You must have known that old reprobate would create like hell when he found his prize apple missing, and why take them from a private garden when we are surrounded by orchards?"

I told him the truth about how Phil Landers had seen this enormous apple and couldn't resist the chance to snatch such a prize. But when we realized the amount of damage this would cause, we had made arrangements to get the thing back to the Colonel, in time for him to put it in the show.

"So what happened?" he asked.

When I told him about the plan that had been scuppered by sabotage to our raft he shouted, "What did you say? Your raft was scuppered, by whom?"

I had gone too far and I knew it, but it was too late now so I told him the whole story about how the Brimly boys had cut through the ropes holding the raft together in such a way that it would break apart once we were out in the current of the river. I explained how this had led to the loss of all our equipment, and the Colonel's apple, which they had grabbed and run off with.

My dad sat on my bed in silence for a while, so I went on eating my tea, nervously looking at him. Finally he said "What you have told me is very serious indeed, I checked that raft and it was well constructed, I was proud of you all for the way you had done it, and I couldn't understand why it had broken apart the way it did. I know you said about hitting an underwater obstruction but even that didn't sound right to me. Now you tell me that some boys from across the river put your lives in danger by destroying your raft, in a way that would only happen when you were out in the fast flowing current?"

I just nodded at this, though none of us had looked at it in quite this way before. We had lost our raft, our stores, and had got soaking wet. But the only thing we wanted was revenge against the boys we knew were responsible.

"I will be having a word with Constable Thackery about this."

I was immediately alarmed and cried out, "No dad please, we know who did it and we want to get our own back on them. We were alright in the water because we're all good swimmers. We want to build another raft and complete the trip. It's our fight when it comes to the Brimlys, and Davie is already working out how we can get back at them."

He looked at me silently for a few minutes and must have seen the desperation in my face.

"Alright, but let me know what you have in mind before you do it and that goes for the whole gang, do you understand?"

I nodded at this, before plucking up the courage to ask him about the loan of four barrels from the pub for the new raft. I was surprised when he smiled, and agreed to it.

"You can have the barrels. We've got too many down in the yard anyway. But don't make your plans yet, I've got to convince your mother this is a good idea first. She didn't like it the first time and after what happened she's not going to be overjoyed at the prospect of you trying it again."

As he went out of the bedroom carrying my tray he turned at the door and winked at me.

"Don't worry, I'll think of a way to get round her."

The next day we met early and all of us had the same story to tell. None of us were sitting very comfortably after the hidings we had suffered the night before. We knew by now how the loud, red faced blowhard, Colonel Worthington-Pugh had found out who pinched his prize apple. It could only be those charming nerks from Brimly. Not content to just destroy our raft and take the apple from us, they then contrived to let everyone in our village know it was us who scrumped it in the first place.

We were a totally dejected lot as we sat there and we had to report to the village hall by ten o'clock. What a trial that was, all of our parents were there, as well as the Reverend, Miss Trump, the Bumstead sisters and the Colonel. They looked at us as though we were criminals going to the gallows, but we had only pinched an apple from this old has-beens garden. It was hardly the crime of the century was it? Unfortunately for us it went against the tradition of the village and retribution would have to be seen to be done.

The Colonel was glaring down at us and suddenly roared out, "You terrible thieves, if you were in the army, under my command, your feet wouldn't touch the ground. It would be the guardhouse for you."

"Alright Colonel," my dad replied, "you're not in the army now and they haven't actually done anything bad. After all boys have been scrumping apples since the dawn of time. Even Adam couldn't resist it in the Garden of Eden, and don't tell me you didn't do it when you were their age."

At this the Colonel made a queer choking sound and spluttered before getting the words out. Nobody had spoken to him like this in a long time. He had become used to men instantly obeying his every word. To have a public servant, which is how he viewed my father, speak to him in this fashion was nowhere near acceptable. But dad stuck to his ground, he wasn't scared of this ex-army officer and was not about to be brow beaten by him.

"I know they took what was supposed to be your prize apple but it's what boys do. Now they have been punished by each of their parents so you can back off."

"I want justice," yelled the Colonel,

"And you'll get it," my dad firmly replied, "they will all come and do whatever work you need doing in your garden, and will be available to everyone else in the village that needs jobs done, for the next week. After that they will have paid their dues and this whole episode can be put firmly out of sight."

I listened to this in fascination. I knew my dad was a strict disciplinarian and had felt the weight of his hand many times, but each time he punished me for something I shouldn't have done. He alone made me realize the difference between right and wrong, but here was a side of him I hadn't seen before. He knew we had all received punishment, and was standing up for us to the whole village, that day I loved my dad more than I ever knew I could.

It was agreed at this meeting, we were going to be very busy for the whole of the next week. The Bumstead sisters put in a claim for our services as did the Reverend Morley. First though we had to report to the home of the preposterous Colonel Worthington-Pugh. He greeted us with a sneer on his face and listed all the things he wanted doing in his garden. Apples to be picked from the trees, packed in straw, and placed in boxes in the shed. All the fallers picked up and the ones that could be saved packed with the rest. He also wanted his lawn mowed and weeded.

This was daunting, but we got stuck in, and in a shorter time than any of us expected, managed to complete most of these tasks. It would have been alright if the Colonel had left us alone to get on with the job, but we had to listen to his stories about the war, especially his boys, the brave men who went into battle under his command. According to him they all loved him but we had our doubts about that.

The way he spoke about his army days was boring and repetitive. Some of this we had heard at least four times before, but we dutifully listened and made the right comments about how thrilling it must have been. We knew the debt the whole of our country owed to people like him who had met the might of the German menace in the last war, and won freedom for us and the rest of the world as a result. It was just the way he tried to tell it, always breaking out into that loud ‘haw haw haw’ laugh.

The time was livened up for us though when Lieutenant Commander Phillips came out into his garden. He leaned on the dividing fence and chatted, and we stopped working to listen to him. His stories really were exciting, and they were always new ones. The Commander held us spellbound as he told of the thunder of guns from our mighty battleships, as they fought against German and Italian ships in the battle for the Atlantic. The fight against the dreaded German U boats, and the way we devised a magnificent underwater detection device that brought so much success to the Allied cause.

While he was telling us these thrilling stories he was rudely interrupted by the Colonel, who came rushing out shouting.

"Kindly do not interrupt these boys Commander, they are here under punishment."

At this Commander Phillips looked crestfallen.

"Sorry Colonel you're quite right, they should be whipped, as well as made to work until they drop for pinching your little apple."

"Little apple," spluttered the Colonel, "it was the biggest one for miles around and would have beaten your pathetic effort easily if these boys hadn't taken it from me."

"Come on Colonel," said the Commander. "Yours wouldn't even have made a half decent pie, whilst mine, the one that actually won first prize, was a corker."

I had heard grown-ups use the expression dancing with rage many times before, it was just part of the language as far as I was concerned. Today though, I saw this in action, the Colonel did dance up and down, his face going redder and redder as his temper mounted. He was calling his distinguished next door neighbour names that none of us had even heard before, and to be calling an ex-Royal Navy officer these embarrassed us a lot.

Commander Phillips, however, thought the whole thing hugely funny, his habit of baiting the Colonel had worked again, as it had on many previous occasions. We heard him laughing still, long after he had gone back inside and closed the door behind him. Now with the Commander out of sight, the Colonel turned his temper on to us.

"You boys don't just stand there, I want the lawn tidied and more weeding done, it doesn't look to me as if you've touched my herbaceous border yet."

With this he stormed off towards his own back door, but turned and looked back just as Davie and Mickie Tranter were making rude gestures in his direction. This proved to be great for us because he went completely haywire and chased us all out of his garden shouting that our parents would hear about this rudeness, and we would never dare come near his house again.

We ran all the way to our forest hideout and spent the rest of the afternoon swimming, climbing and laughing at what had happened. Phil Landers, who was a very good mimic, had us all in stitches as he shoved one of our cushions up his jumper, and gave a near perfect impersonation of the red faced, chubby, Colonel Worthington-Pugh.

Our parents had been informed, by the still furious army officer, of what had taken place on his very own property. He had been assured by eight sets of parents that the offending boys would hear more about this when they get home. It was my mum who told me off, but she couldn't keep a straight face when I told her what Commander Phillips had said to him, and then described the gestures made by Davie and Mickie after he had shouted so much at us.

"It was very wrong of you," she said, before turning through into the public bar where my father was. He too saw the funny side, I heard him roar with laughter and he said "That'll teach the old bugger."

We were then in good spirits as we prepared to tackle the last two days of our week of punishment. With just over a week to go before school started again, we wanted to get back to really enjoying the rest of the glorious summer. Our first port of call today was to the village hall, which was used twice a week for sports.

Arriving there we had to report to Maud, the first of the Bumstead sisters, a large frowning woman who, if anything, was even louder than the robust riding school leader Ada. She didn't like men and would have nothing whatsoever to do with any of them. If she even saw a man she would cross the road, changing direction altogether to avoid any conflict. She seldom came into our pub because my dad was behind the bar and most of the village men were there every evening. There was probably a reason for this seemingly peculiar behaviour, but if our parents knew what it was they certainly didn't share this information.

Now this lady was glaring at us. In her eyes we were, of course, junior versions of men and so she didn't like us either. She spent as little time as possible in our company, preferring to just shout at us. "Clean this hall from top to bottom, I want the whole place swept and dusted. The windows need cleaning, they're filthy, so get on with it, then get out of my sight."

Charming, we like you too, we thought and this time all of us were making rude gestures as soon as her back was turned.

The sweeping and dusting was easy, for the window cleaning though, we needed buckets of warm soapy water. It was a boring job so, inevitably, most of this landed on us leaving six fairly clean windows and eight soaking wet, but very happy boys. We could have left straight away, but as we turned to go, Danny Meadows was looking out of the nearest window.

"Wha, look at that." We all came to see and stood looking out at the sports field behind the hall. This was where we would be playing cricket against our arch rivals the Brimly schoolboys in two weeks time.

Today though, Miss Maud Bumstead was roaring on a bunch of rugby players, but not the usual ones we would expect to see. These were all teenage girls, and to us they looked completely daft in rugby shirts and men's shorts. The Bumstead voice boomed out over the field.

"Come on Sheila push harder you'll never get the ball that way, and Gloria what on earth do you think you're doing? This is a scrum down, bend into it and push."

We looked at this in total amazement, though soccer was our game we would watch the Surlington men whenever they played rugby, and had seen England play on the Pathe news at the fleapit cinema. We knew that physical strength as well as skill was needed to play this tough game. Men didn't have bulges in the front of their shirts either, but some of these girls had very big bulges indeed.

It was so funny we collapsed with laughter which brought the redoubtable Miss Bumstead into the hall to chase us out. Still laughing as we ran away, that great voice echoed behind us.

"You men, you're all the same, but you don't rule the world. Our day is coming, when women will have their rights."

What was the silly woman raving about? What rights? I would have to ask my dad in private tonight.

Now there was the other Miss Bumstead to contend with, so we walked across the village, then along the pony trail until we came to the riding stable. This was very well kept, and provided beginners lessons, rides in the forest beyond Banter Wood and pony and trap rides through the large and lovely woodland. We weren't greeted any more warmly by Ada Bumstead than we had been by her sister. All of the tack used for the horses in their various duties, including leather bridles and saddles, had to be cleaned, and the brass work on the pony traps used for the visitors, needed polishing.

The result of this work may have been good, but it was not a job that ten year old boys enjoyed doing, especially when we were supposed to be enjoying our summer holidays. We moaned about it as we worked , even when two of Miss Bumstead's 'gels' came into the tack room it made no difference to us.

They were nice, attractive girls, as my dad frequently said, but I couldn't see why he and most of the other men in the village seemed to go all funny when they rode by on their horses. I didn't even think they looked like girls at all because they wore the silliest looking tight trousers, called jodhpurs, high length leather boots, and what looked like motor bike crash helmets on their heads. They took no notice of us as they collected the equipment they needed for one of the ponies, which was soon placed in the shafts of one of the traps. Once lead outside, the pony and trap stood waiting, ready to provide another forest ride for the visitors.

Mickie Tranter was a very big fan of cowboy films and never missed going to see them when they were showing at the fleapit. His hero was Roy Rogers, the singing cowboy, though when Mickie tried to copy him the result was a horrible noise. He was a great lad and a true friend, but never a singer. He also liked Gene Autry, and Lash Laroo.

Now as the boredom of the job we were doing began to settle in, he gazed out towards the yard, and his eyes settled on the waiting pony. In a flash he left the tack room, got into the trap, and then grasped the reins with a loud 'Git up thar' just as his cowboys said in the films. The pony, which had been standing quietly, was startled at this strange command, and the result was horrendous. It reared up on its hind legs, let out a loud neighing sound then took off towards the gate of the riding stable yard.

Mickie was thrown back, but he struggled up and started pulling back on the reins shouting 'woe.' The pony took no notice, making a headlong dash towards the field on the other side of the lane from the stables. Where this drama would have ended is anybody's guess, but fortunately for all concerned, the farmer who owned the field was working in it with two of his men. Being experienced with horses they knew just what to do in a situation like this, so they stood waving their arms above their heads in front of the madly bolting pony. Stopping quickly in its tracks it reared onto its hind legs again, but quick as a flash the farmer grabbed the bridle. By speaking quietly, and stroking the now trembling pony, he was able to bring the whole thing to a stop.

An outraged Miss Bumstead, with all of her gels in tow, arrived in the field. We followed at a safe distance, and really worried about what would happen to poor Mickie. If this latest prank got back to the ears of his parents he probably wouldn't be allowed out to play with us for the rest of the holidays.

Miss Bumstead raged at Mickie as he sat in the trap, she called him a vandal and said she would report him to his parents and to the RSPCA for cruelty to her beloved pony, whose name was Pinky. Her girls now had the horse under their care. After roughly ordering Mickie out of the trap they turned Pinky around and led him back to the stables. Miss Bumstead was still shouting at Mickie, telling him what a waste of time small boys were, especially us lot.

"What was I thinking of?" she raged, "getting these useless boys to do anything in my lovely stable. I should have known something like this would happen."

Mickie was sitting on the ground while all of this was going on. His usual happy face was now clouded by the insults coming from this awful woman. She may not like boys, but we weren't over fond of her either, or her sister. We couldn't tell her this though, because that would have been regarded as cheek and once again our parents would have been told.

"Just what did you think you were doing you awful boy?" she yelled.

Before Mickie could answer, and what he would have said I do not know, Davie intervened.

"Please Miss, it wasn't his fault, I knocked my bucket over and it made the horse jump so much he just bolted. Mickie jumped into the trap and tried to stop him before he got to the gate."

"Nonsense," she said. "It would take more than a dropped bucket to startle my lovely Pinky, you must have done something really wicked to make him bolt like that."

We were crestfallen now because it was becoming increasingly obvious that the stable owner was not going to believe anything we told her. It was the farmer who came to our rescue.

"In fairness Ma'am, the lad was trying to stop the pony and it was only his lack of strength that prevented him from doing it. From where I was standing I think you owe him a vote of thanks."

Miss Bumstead glared at him, but didn't want to get into an argument with a fully grown man, so she turned and quite literally stamped her way back to the riding stable. Her parting words faded into the distance, telling us what would happen if we ever came near her darling horses again. This of course suited us very well and as we turned to leave we thanked the farmer for his help.

"It was a pleasure boys," then looking at Mickie, "the next time you stir up a horse like that young fellow, make sure you know how to handle it."

Then with a wink at all of us he went back to his work.

"He knew all the time," said a delighted Mickie Tranter.

"Yeah," said Davie, "and it looks like he's not too fond of Miss flipping Ada Bumstead either."

Our last port of call to finish what we considered to be a harsh punishment week was at the village church. Fifteenth century and with a huge spire, it was a building we knew very well indeed, spending most of every Sunday inside it. We had to report to the Reverend Morley to see what he wanted us to do. We saw him from the choir stalls at each Sunday service. He had been the vicar here for longer than any of us had been alive, at least twenty two years. He was a well built man, who was completely bald on the top of his head.

I had so much trouble every week when he stood out in front of the congregation conducting the service. I knew it was wrong to laugh in church but looking at him I couldn't help it. He would be solemnly preaching the Word of God, but from where we were sitting we could see the lights overhead and the candles on the altar reflecting in his shiny bald spot. My dad wasn't particularly religious, by my mum certainly was, and if she knew I laughed in church I would be for it, but what could I do? We were boys and found things like that funny, even though this wasn't really right since it was not his fault. He was good at his job though, and young as we were we all knew that.

Nothing in his parish was ever too much trouble for him, and all of the villagers, not only in Surlington, but the whole surrounding area, could come to him for help at any time. One thing worried me though, I had heard things like baldness were hereditary, and once I found out what that word meant, things that parents had may be passed on to their children, I looked at my father. Fortunately for me he had a full head of dark brown hair that showed no sign of falling out. As he was now, at thirty six, fairly old, I became confident that going bald was not something I should be worrying about.

We were met at the church hall by the round figure of the vicar's wife. We all liked Mrs Morley. She was fun and always had a few words to say to us after each service we officiated at. To us it was just helping out, but we learned this word from the studious Danny Meadows, who heard his dad saying it, and thought it sounded good. She greeted us all warmly and told us she would like the prayer and hymn books dusted, and then stacked neatly into one of the cupboards at the back of the hall. This should be done on a regular basis, but there was never enough time on a Sunday after all three services had finished. So they were just packed into piles at the back of the church, then placed anywhere in the hall on Monday.

She could tell from our expressions we were not overjoyed at this job. We had done this sort of thing twice in the past two days and frankly were fed up with it. We should have been out in Banter Wood, climbing trees, swimming in the river and enjoying ourselves instead. Boring jobs like cleaning and dusting was what our mother's did at home. Mrs Morley winked at us though.

"Don't worry. I'll bring you something to eat while you're working."

This cheered us up straight away, Mrs Morley was well known in the whole area for her wonderful cooking just as much as the way she helped her husband with his church work. Every time there was a show or garden fete, her pies, cakes and pastries were the centre of attention. We did indeed cheer up at the thought of what she would bring out for us.

The books were dusted, well shaken up a bit anyway, in double quick time and stacked, if not exactly tidily, at least inside the cupboards by the time she came back.

"Oh well done boys," she said when she came into the hall and there was not a single prayer or hymn book in sight. "You've earned this haven't you?"

She then placed a tray onto one of the small tables which was laden with eight of her delicious meat pies, plus a selection of small cream cakes. We thanked her very much for this then fell on it. In less time than it would take to walk around the outside of the church hall, the tray was empty, and eight happy boys were starting back to Banter Wood to enjoy what was left of our holiday. We would also be planning how we could best get back at our enemies from Brimly village, in a way that would cause them the most embarrassment.

Chapter 5

We were now half way through the fifth week of the summer holidays and school was looming once again. Our parents had taken us into Westbridge, which was a large town just fifteen miles outside of Surlington. This was where most of us would come to get things that are not available in a small village. I had been brought here by my mother to get shoes, trousers, blazer and a cap for the new school year. The rest of the lads had made the same trip with their parents, for the same reason.

Now a year older than the previous time this trip was made we had all grown out of last year's clothes. Most of these cast offs would be taken to the church and given to Mrs Morley. She was always grateful to receive them because she ran a woman's institution that helped out poor and needy families. Our passed on clothes were given to people who didn't have enough money to buy them. The ones our mother's kept were for us to wear as play clothes. We would all be wearing the new clothes at school in just over a week's time.

Upon returning we went again to the hideout and our leader was going over what we hoped to achieve in the time left to us.

"Firstly boys we want to rebuild our raft, and this time nothing is going to stop us going all the way down the Gest as we wanted to do last time. This would have been done if that Brimly lot hadn't sabotaged us. We're going to get our own back on them for that."

This statement was greeted with a large amount of enthusiasm by us all.

I pointed out though that I had to wait for permission from my father to go on the next raft trip. Most of the others agreed with this, they had gone through the same trouble with their own parents when they got home on the day of the sinking.

"Will he let you go?" asked Davie. "I haven't had any trouble with my mum and dad about it."

"I think so," I said, "but he has to get over mum's objections about it."

"How's he going to do that?" asked Phil Landers. "Your mum's not easy to convince."

"How do you know that?" I asked, somewhat startled at this statement about my mother.

"My dad said so," he replied. "He said that anyone causing trouble in your pub had to be more wary of her than your dad."

I was surprised to hear this, but also quite proud. If the men of the village were wary of upsetting my mum then she went up even more in my estimation, which of course was already very high indeed. I was at the same time a little worried about how dad was going to get round her to enable me to go on the next voyage of adventure down the mighty, raging, River Gest.

"Alright," said Davie loudly. "We'll deal with any problems in that department when we have to. But we can get on with building the next raft whatever happens. Now I have spoken to David Callow and offered him the chance to join our gang."

"Is he going to?" I asked.

"I don't know yet," Davie said. "He didn't seem all that interested when I asked him."

We found this not only strange, but also slightly insulting. We wouldn't just ask anyone to join our exclusive gang. It was an honour, and we didn't understand how he would not straight away jump at the chance to join the most elite gang in the whole district. So there were loud shouts of dissent over this and Davie had to shout to restore order.

"It's not that he doesn't want to join us," he said. "As you all know he's in the scouts, and he's only just got back from their annual summer camp. He goes to meetings twice a week in that rundown old scout hut of theirs. He also plays football for Surlington boys under fifteens, as well as cricket for the village junior team. But he is coming here tomorrow and we'll tell him why we want him to join us, and if he agrees then he'll be in."

"Not without passing the initiation test first," said Phil Landers.

There was a chorus of assent about this because to be a Sundance gang member, it was very important that you could and would do anything necessary to uphold the honour and traditions of the gang. To this end the initiation ceremony challenged the new recruit to do things that would always end in complete embarrassment.

"Not the full initiation," said Davie. "We haven't got time for one thing and we want him in the gang helping with the raft."

"Yes I know," I said, "but he's got to pass at least one test so I propose trial by water."

This was greeted by a lot of laughter, because David Callow's mum was well known in the village. She ironed everything that he, his sister and his dad wore so that even in play clothes David's shirts and short trousers had sharp creases in them. His scout uniform was also ironed perfectly every time he set out. We were neatly turned out, at least for part of the time, before we got into one game or another where we always ended up getting soaking wet or very creased and crumpled.

Next morning Davie arrived in the wood accompanied by a slightly nervous David Callow. To look at him I couldn't understand how a boy of his age could look so neat and tidy. Even his shoes were polished, and his socks, coming up to just below his knees were held there by garters his mum made for him. Our socks, by comparison were always down around our ankles and we were always being told, both at home and at school to pull them up.

"Alright David," said Davie. "You know everyone here and they will all be pleased to welcome you into the gang, but as I explained to you there is a test for you to pass first."

"Yes I know that, and that's what's worrying me," David replied.

"There's nothing to worry about," we all told him, but from the way he looked at us he clearly didn't believe us. We started off into the depths of Banter Wood to the wide stream that flowed through before emptying into the River Gest. It was deep enough for us to both swim and dive in and we did a lot of both every summer. Today we were all fully dressed and obviously not planning to do any swimming.

We came first to the rope hanging from a branch of one of the huge oak trees. We had endless fun swinging out on this and dropping straight into the water. Today though the challenge was to see who could swing out the furthest without falling off. This was managed with ease, some of us swinging out almost to the opposite bank before coming back onto dry land again.

When it was David's turn however we wouldn't let him land, we just kept telling him to try again to get further out. Inevitably he lost his hold on the rope and with an almighty splash landed in the water. Returning to the bank he didn't look as neat and tidy as when he had first joined us this morning. His clothes were soaking wet and there was no sign of his mother's carefully ironed creases. He stood there in front of us and spluttered.

"You did that on purpose, just look at me."

"Yeah I know," said Davie, "but it's all a part of the test, and don't worry you'll soon dry out."

He did eventually, but not before he had been ducked several more times. We challenged him to walk the tightrope across the one bridge over this stream, which incidentally was known to us all as 'The River'. We did this all the time, balancing on one side of the parapet. We were all used to it and found it easy, but because he wasn't, and we were shaking it from our side, he fell off.

Crossing the stream lower down, over the fallen tree trunk that was green and slimy in the middle and David fell off again. It went on like that all morning and when we came back to our hideout all of us including David were in very high spirits indeed. He had actually come to enjoy himself as he plunged so many times into the water. Before this he always had to be so careful about his clothes. Now though, they were so wrinkled he looked just like a boy of his age should look and we all, unanimously, voted him into the Sundance Gang.

His mother, predictably, had a fit when she saw him, but we'd all practiced what he should tell her. That a swan was caught in weeds in the river and was in danger of drowning. So being a boy scout, David had leaped into the water to save it. Swans are big powerful birds and to attempt a rescue operation like that would mean the person involved would get not only very wet but roughed up a lot as well. In David's case it worked, his mum stopped shouting at him and even gave him a special tea as a treat that night.

The next day the rebuilding of the raft was planned in the secrecy of our hideout. Our new member was holding forth, telling us about the various methods his fellow scouts came up with on their annual raft racing day. He wanted to combine two designs. Our idea for the last one, with sturdy logs, tied securely together was to be bolstered by another cradle with a barrel at each corner.

"That's your department Billy," Davie told me. "What's the news on the barrels?"

"It's ok," I replied. "My dad said we can have what we want, but there are conditions."

"What conditions?" they all wanted to know.

"Well like I told you dad had to get round my mum before he could let me have another go on a raft, and it wasn't easy for him."

This was true, just two nights before dad had come into my room to tell me I could go on the raft, and have the barrels we needed, but only if we were all wearing life jackets. Mum really was worried about our safety and this was something she wasn't going to give way on. When I told the others this they wondered just where these were going to come from. Several of their parents had talked about life jackets as well, so they weren't surprised to hear my mum wanted us protected in this way.

Dad had arranged to get nine life jackets for us.

"Ted Bancroft, an old friend of mine from school days has a ships chandlers over in Westbridge and has agreed to lend them to me for you all to wear," he told me.

"What's a ships chandlers?" I had wondered.

"It's a place that deals with everything a ship needs before setting out to sea, that means food and equipment like ropes, chains, anchors and all that sort of thing."

I also wanted to know about the peculiar remark made by Miss Maud Bumstead when she chased us out of the village hall. I told him she was shouting about women getting their rights.

"Take no notice of her Billy. She's got these daft ideas about women being equal to men. In some ways they are, and we certainly couldn't do without them. Where would you be without your mother for instance? But to suggest they could compete with us in anything we do is just plain stupid. Girls playing rugby for instance, ridiculous."

He had been laughing all the way back downstairs.

Davie and the others were very pleased. With our enthusiasm and David Callow's knowledge, the new raft would soon be underway. It would take us over a week to build though, which meant we would be back at school before it was finished. Then we would only have weekends to work on it properly. Also coming up was the harvest, a big thing in a farming community like ours, and we would be very much involved in this.

We spent the last week of the holidays working on the new raft, as well as playing all of our favourite games in the wonderful surroundings of Banter Wood. The whole gang, including our new member had turned up at the Dog and Duck and with my dad's permission rolled four barrels away. Two boys to each one and with Davie our leader showing the way he was able to get out of the rolling duties. We took these to our hideout ready for use and left them out of sight behind our bird hide. The rest of that week went so fast that before we realised it we were being woken up and told to get up and get ready for school.

Then, with not a lot of enthusiasm we set off for the familiar playground of the village school. Resplendent in our new clothes we met up with our headmistress Miss Tuttle. She greeted us all as she usually did, setting out what she hoped we would achieve in the coming academic year. She also reminded us in the top year that we would be taking the scholarship at the end of it, and the results of this would determine where we would be going to finish our education.

None of us were looking forward to this. If we passed we would go on to attend the very posh grammar school two miles outside of Westbridge. Having heard all sorts of horror stories about this school and what they expected of their pupils we didn't want to go there. They won sports prizes the like of which we could never hope to achieve. They also expected their pupils to be very high achievers in the education stakes. We weren't dunces, but we weren't knowledge bumps either.

We wanted something like the school we were attending now, with a mistress like Miss Tuttle. Although we couldn't fool her, and we tried on so many occasions, we all liked her. Yes she shouted at us, and caned us if we really misbehaved, but she was fair as well. We could go to her if we were in any sort of trouble and she would listen and always offer advice that helped. If we could get just enough marks in this important exam we would go on to Lipton Comprehensive. This was two miles down the road from the grammar school, and was in Westbridge itself. But our parents would provide transport to get us there and we would all stay together.

As that first assembly came to a close, with the school anthem of Greensleeves, I was looking at Miss Trout. I had seen her on the sports field so many times before and had not taken any notice. But having seen the girls training for rugby at Miss Bumstead's sports lessons, something had awakened in me. Those teenage girls had big bulges in their shirts and that excited me. I was instantly reminded of how Miss Trout looked even better when she came out onto our sports field, leading out whatever girl's class she was taking that day. She had lovely long legs and she too had big bulges in the tight top she wore.

Our girls, I always thought looked ridiculous. When we turned out for sports we wore shorts and vests. The girls simply had to tuck their blouses into navy blue knickers that reached almost to their knees, and that did nothing at all for any of us.

Today as Miss Trout looked out over assembly from the raised stage at the front of the hall, she smiled at us. But I thought she was smiling just at me and I had the most peculiar feeling in my body. I actually felt weak at the knees. Just thinking of Miss Trout from that morning on, and for the rest of our time in this school, I had these same feelings coursing through me but no idea why this was happening. I made the mistake of telling Davie about this and he just laughed at me.

"Oh no, don't tell me we've got another soppy pants, and with a teacher too. You're mad Billy."

So that was that, my feelings for the lovely Miss Trout became my own secret.

The first thing we had to organise was the cricket match against Brimly. We met in the hall after school on the third day of our first week back to discuss our team for this important game. Mr Gardener, our sports master was in charge and he started by reminding us of what had happened at last year's game at their school.

"Now then boys, we know what we'll be up against in this match. Brimly school have a very good team as we saw last year. They have some very good batsmen and they are very fast when running between the wickets. I'm sure I don't have to remind any of you of their tactic of hitting the ball out of range into the wooded surrounds of their sports field. While you were all looking for it they ran thirty eight runs. That's why we lost the match by a humiliatingly large score. We must be on our guard against anything like that happening at this year's fixture on our own ground."

We were all in agreement over this, because we were still smarting from the game last year. The Brimly's had thought the whole thing so funny that the next day, after the match, we found a big banner outside of our playground that simply said '*thirty eight*'. We wanted revenge so our team had to be the best eleven we could put on the field. This may be sound judgement but it was complicated by the fact that only one or two of our boys were actually any good at this game.

David Callow was brilliant, an all round player, good with the bat, and a very good fast bowler as well. Apart from him though we only had Davie Collins and Martin Ashford, who were likely to make runs for us. We were not much better at fielding either, but we did have Joe Carter, a very good wicket keeper.

As for myself I enjoyed going to the fleapit to watch England playing Test Cricket, and listened spell bound to the commentary by the legendary John Arlott on the wireless. We admired all of the team. They had just completed a three-one test series win against a very strong South African team, led by an amazing cricketer, Len Hutton. He had played magnificently in England's losing ashes series in Australia during the winter and now guided this great team of ours, which also had the famous Denis Compton and Alec Bedser, to a great win against very stern opposition.

On the twenty third of August my dad had given me a wonderful surprise when he said I could bring one friend with me if I would like to go to Southampton with him to watch South Africa take on Hampshire at their small, but famous County Ground. Naturally I jumped at the chance and nominated Davie Collins to come as well. The County Ground is situated only a very short distance from Southampton football clubs ground. This is called the Dell, and we had to pass this before turning into Northlands Road where the cricket ground was to be found.

It was a wonderful day and the cricket was so thrilling to watch. A Test team playing against a county team, and the standard we saw that day was breathtaking. I watched in total fascination as these professional players stroked the ball around the park. While the fielders and bowlers were also so good, it put me in the shade. We went home that day happy and grateful to my dad for taking us.

Now, back at our team meeting I had to realise once again that I would be picked to play. Not because I was any good at all, but simply to make up the numbers. My trouble was that I was no good at batting, was hopeless at fielding, had no idea how to bowl and would never even be considered as a wicket keeper. Unfortunately this also applied to a few more of our players. So our team had to rely on just two or three players to get enough runs, and to get the other team out when they were batting.

On the day the Brimly team won the toss and elected to bat first. Their openers were their captain Frank Thornton and Bob Yates. Both of these were very good with the bat so it was important for us to get them out quickly. In the second over

Frank whacked the ball high into the air, and with cries of "catch it" ringing in my ears I went for glory and got right underneath as it returned to earth. It was a straight forward catch so quite how I managed to miss it was something nobody could explain afterwards. It dropped at least two feet clear of my outstretched hands and went to ground.

The innings went on like this for the next eight overs with no-one making any impression on the batsman, and the score went to thirty nine for no wicket. That's when it happened. Bob Yates hit a magnificent drive into the rough ground in the woods beyond the boundary. We all rushed after it, but just like last year couldn't find it. This wasn't county cricket where the most a batsman can score from one ball is six. In our game the batsmen keep running until the ball comes back into play. That's how Brimly had scored thirty eight from one ball in last year's game.

"Find it," shouted Davie. "We can't let them beat last year's record."

Responding to the urgency in his voice we frantically looked in the long grass, but there was no sign of that orange cricket ball.

Suddenly Keith Andrews shouted, "It's in the bog."

This was an area of ground that was always muddy, no matter what the weather and we could see the outline of the ball right in the middle of this oozy mud.

"Phil you're the tallest," shouted Davie, "get it out."

Poor Phil, he was resplendent that day in his cricket whites because they had long trousers. He really should be wearing these all the time because as he got older his legs got longer and in short trousers he was beginning to look really daft. Now though he was being told to wade into this odious bog to retrieve a cricket ball. He opened his mouth to protest but was shouted down straight away.

"Do it," ordered Davie. "They've already run sixteen and we must stop them before they get more than last year."

It made perfect sense so Phil stretched his long arms out to try and get the ball. He nearly made it, but just as his hands touched it he lost his balance and fell headfirst into the mud. It would have been good if we could have shown him some sympathy, but the situation was desperate and all he got from us was "throw the ball."

He grabbed it from the clinging mud and threw it to Davie, who rushed out into the open and with his strong right arm threw it to Joe Carter, who expertly took the bails off just as Frank Thornton was running back to complete run number twenty eight.

"Out," said umpire Colonel Worthington-Pugh, and Frank trudged off the field. We were elated, we had stopped them from getting past last year's one ball total and they had made just twenty seven from this year's lost ball.

We basked in the glory of this and it was only poor Phil Landers who was not happy. He had looked really good in his cricket whites, but they were now black with mud all down the front. With Frank Thornton now out the rest of their team were dismissed for another eighteen runs, so they made eighty four. Bob Yates was the only one not out.

We now had a reasonable task to get the runs we needed to win this game and started out very well indeed. Our openers were the very dependable pair of Davie Collins and David Callow. We expected them to do the job for us and they nearly did. The score was sixty five for no wicket when a ball from Frank Thornton went past Davie's bat and knocked his off stump right out of the ground. We then predictably lost four wickets for a measly nine runs.

Seventy four for five the scoreboard now read as I strode to the wicket. We needed ten runs to win and had six overs in which to get them. I managed, more by luck than anything else, to survive the last two balls of Frank Thornton's over. In the next two overs David Callow kept the strike and scored seven of the runs we needed for victory.

Now I stood at the crease and looked towards the big figure of Bill Grimes who was bowling to me. He stood there and glared down the wicket at me, while all around the rest of this odious team were mouthing insults at me. But one thing I have found, both from these days, and later when I grew up, was that I am so much better at anything I do if I am being barracked by the opposition. That day I grew in stature and first of all stood my ground and glared back at Grimes taking no notice of the shouts all around me.

The first two balls he bowled went wide of the wicket and it was easy for me to leave them. It was the third ball that came off my bat and went high in the air, disappearing into the woods out of sight. As the Brimly team rushed to get it back David Callow and I ran as fast as our legs would carry us and gloriously won the game for Surlington. David had scored many more runs than I had, but the four we ran then won the game for us. So it was me who was carried shoulder high from the pitch.

With everyone cheering and making a lot of noise I was over the moon. It was Davie running alongside me who asked why I was holding my right hand.

"It's nothing."

I never told him or anyone else the reason I was holding my hand like that was because my right thumb was hurting badly. When facing that last ball from Bill Grimes I had tried to hit it. But it bounced off the turf in front of me and before I could get out of the way it reared up and hit my thumb. From there it flew away out of sight enabling me and David to get the winning runs.

I would now go down in Surlington folk lore as the boy who hit the winning runs against Brimly. But I never actually hit the ball at all, it hit me. This was to remain my secret though and boy did I enjoy the after match tea, and the admiration of all my team mates.

Even Miss Trout came up to me. "Well done Billy," she said and I nearly feinted. What was it about her that made me feel this way whenever I looked at her, and especially when she spoke to me?

There was the added joy of looking across the hall and smirking at our defeated opponents and Davie had not lost the opportunity of reminding Frank Thornton that we would be seeking revenge for the wrecking of our raft.

"Try what you like," he had replied. "We'll be ready for you. Our boys can do anything better than your pathetic lot."

This insult was passed on to us the next day and our resolve to strike back at the Brimly boys grew even stronger. But we still had no real plan yet. We wanted to do something spectacular, that would cause them embarrassment and make them look like a whole lot of idiots. A good idea but so far not one of us had come up with anything that would bring this about.

Next though was the harvest. Ours was a farming community, so on both sides of the river men and boys from the villages would be out in the fields bringing in the crops. We went straight from school and reported to old Jack Harlow. He had worked on Mosely Farm for many years, starting as a farm hand for Mr Wakefield such a long time ago. Now he looked after all of the livestock and was working for the original Mr Wakefield's grandson Len. This year he had been appointed as Lord of the Harvest. It was up to him to see that everything was gathered in properly, and he who delegated the jobs.

Overalls were put on over our clothes before jumping up into the carts that would carry the sheaves of wheat away from the fields to be built into haystacks. The grownups would throw these up and it was our job to stack them neatly. We had wonderful meals, brought out to all the labourers by the village women, my mum included. We sat with the men eating cheese and pickle with huge chunks of bread. The men had bottles of beer to drink, while we had lemonade.

These days of gathering the harvest were always hard work, but so enjoyable. The camaraderie between everyone involved was incredible and even we, as young as we were, appreciated this. At Turvy Mill some of the village woman had been hard at work baking the special loaves that would be displayed in the church. These were traditional and were baked every year for this purpose in the shape of haystacks. This was a very busy time for us. Apart from helping in the fields we had to report to Miss Trump for choir practice.

The harvest festival service was one of the highlights of the year. The church was decorated with all sorts of local produce that had either been gathered or picked. After the service it would be packed into small bundles and distributed to the needy of the parish. We had to give our best from the choir stalls so Miss Trump had us practicing the three hymns that were always sung at this service, 'We plough the fields and scatter', 'Come ye thankful people come' and 'All things bright and beautiful'.

We sang these over and over again until she was satisfied. It was on the last practice that everyone, including Miss Trump, was surprised when the door opened and the portly figure of Colonel Worthington-Pugh came into the room.

"Excuse me Ma'am, I heard the boys singing as I went past and couldn't resist coming in."

"That's quite alright Colonel," said Miss Trump. "Please come and join us."

We didn't know what to make of this. The last time we had seen this man we had been running away from his garden with him shouting after us. Why would he suddenly just turn up here? It was well known in the village that he never attended church services. We went on with the practice and gave voice once again to 'Come, ye thankful people'. After finishing the hymn the army officer seemed to be crying.

"Are you alright Colonel?" our choir mistress anxiously asked him. He looked up at her as he wiped his eyes.

"Yes Miss Trump, I'm alright, it's just that listening to these boys singing such a lovely hymn brings back memories of a time when the world had gone mad. It reminded me of June 1940. I, along with two hundred men under my command was on the beaches of Dunkirk. We had been fighting Hitler's troops in France. Unfortunately for us they were stronger and better armed than we were. Over three thousand British expeditionary troops were forced onto those beaches and we had to wait to be rescued. I remember most of all the Sunday before we got off the beaches and came home. It was church parade and the parson had just been preaching to us about the goodness of man, and God being on our side. Then we heard the whine of aircraft and they fired at us. So many men kneeling in prayer were mercilessly mown down. Over thirty of my own men included. If it hadn't been for the bravery of the Navy, and the men who came in their own boats, none of us would have got off.

I have never seen such a huge array of assorted boats. From Royal Navy destroyers to small fishing boats, they came, and kept coming until most of us had been lifted from the shore and carried across the channel to this country. But from that dreadful day to this I have never been able to forgive God for letting that happen to so many good men. They were family men, and now their children have to grow up without them. And it happened while they were praying, while they were actually speaking to him."

There was an awkward silence after this. We were seeing a side of the Colonel none of us knew anything at all about. Looking at him now we could see how he held that rank. I knew all about Dunkirk because two of my uncles from my mother's side of the family had their own fishing boat. They made a reasonable living before the war, catching and selling fresh fish in and around the villages. When the call went out from the Navy to commandeer as many small craft as possible, they had volunteered not only their boat but their services as well. They made countless crossings to Dunkirk and back, bringing our soldiers home. On the last trip they made my Uncle Donald was hit by bullets from a German plane and killed outright.

His brother Keith brought the boat back, even though he too had been hit in the leg. My mother had told me about this as my uncle Keith never mentioned his brother to me. He still fishes in the same boat, but mum said his whole personality changed that day after the loss he suffered off the beaches of Dunkirk.

Miss Trump now looked with sympathy at the Colonel. "But you went back on D-Day and drove the German's out of Europe."

"Yes we did, and so many of my men who survived Dunkirk were with me as we stormed ashore onto Gold Beach, and drove inland. I didn't have to lecture them about what I expected of them once we got ashore, they knew. For them this was their chance to avenge their comrades who had died four years before without mercy from the enemy they had come to defeat."

Miss Trump smiled at him then startled us all.

"Won't you join the boys in singing a hymn Colonel?"

At first he was as surprised as we were, but then, incredibly he said, "Thank you ma'am, I think I'd like that."

So we made room for him and started again singing 'Come ye thankful people come'. It felt unreal. All of our combined voices were being drowned out by the loud voice of the Colonel. He sang that hymn with such feeling that even we were impressed. We broke up after that and went home, talking as we went about this new side of a person who until now we had thought of as a figure of fun.

The following Sunday all of us were in church for the big harvest festival service. Reverend Morley told us as we were helping with the displays to make sure all the apples go round the altar, not in any of our pockets. This was unfair. Yes we scrumped other peoples apples whenever we got the chance, but none of us would take harvest produce from the church. The Reverend though just winked at us so we knew he was joking.

Just as the service was about to start there was a small disturbance at the back of the church as the big doors were opened. Most of the congregation turned to see why this was and there was a gasp as the Colonel entered. He stood, awkwardly looking around him, and it was my dad who moved up in his pew and said, "Colonel, come and sit here."

He came over and sat through the whole service next to my parents. A new dawn had begun and we were to find there was a lot more to this rather remarkable man than any of us had ever realised.

Chapter 6

Now the harvest was over we could get back to our school work. The dreaded scholarship was still at the back of our minds even though it wasn't until the start of next year's summer holiday. We would have exams in everything except crafts, which for us were woodwork and metalwork, and for the girls, cookery and needlework.

At our first woodwork lesson of the new term Mr Bond told us that now we were in the top year we should be thinking about things that were more difficult to make.

"Working with wood is a good thing to be able to do," he told us. He asked how the things that were finished and taken home at the end of the summer term had turned out. I was less than truthful with my answer.

"How did your mother like that toast rack you made Billy? Is she using it?"

"Yes Sir," I lied.

In fact she had tried but the very first time she actually put some toast into it the silly thing fell apart. I put this down to bad glue, but my dad just laughed. "Never mind Billy, we can't all be good carpenters." For me this was certainly true.

I did love helping out with the new raft though and did my share in its construction. This was coming along very nicely indeed. The first stage was complete with nine stout logs tied securely together. David Callow had checked this at every stage to make sure everything was being properly done. We were now working on the carriage underneath where support would be provided by four barrels, one at each corner. She was already looking much sturdier than our first raft and we were really looking forward to going down the river.

This time we would have a real sail as well, one of the local farmers had given us a big piece of cloth and we were delighted with this. Once we had fixed the mast in place we would get the help of some of our girls to fashion the sail for us. We had been surprised when Angela Ford, along with her best friend Francis Cooper had approached us with this idea.

"Why do you want to help?" asked a bemused Davie. "This is a boy's job."

"Oh is it? How many of you can use scissors properly and sew?"

There was only one answer to that, none of us had ever attempted to use a needle before, that's why we all had mothers.

But at the next gang meeting this situation had to be seriously discussed. It was firmly pointed out that above the door of our hideout were those immortal words *No Girls Allowed.* The Sundance Gang was for boys only. Just like so many Gentlemen's clubs around the country, especially in London, where women were not allowed to pass through the front door. Even Lords, the most famous cricket ground in the world, did not allow women to enter the sacred long room. For our girls to make our sail they would have to come here.

"Yes I know that," said Davie. "But they can only go in the clearing where the raft is moored, they can't come in here."

We still weren't happy with this. Even the clearing next to our hideout was too close for most of us. Angela and Frances had put up a strong argument about this however, even putting forward a plan to make sure the Brimly gang wouldn't be able to sabotage our raft as they had done last time.

But, as Davie said, we could at least hear them out.

So on a day that will go down in Surlington boys history, Angela Ford and Frances Cooper came into Banter Wood and approached the bird hide headquarters of the Sundance Gang. As they entered the clearing Davie met them and said, “That’s far enough.”

“What do you mean?” said Angela.

“I mean that’s far enough,” said Davie, “if you look at the door of our hideout you will see it says no girls allowed.”

“That’s daft,” they both said together.

“What are you afraid of?” asked Frances. “Do you think we’re not as good as you?”

“It’s not that,” replied Davie, “it’s a long standing club rule.”

Actually this was what we all really thought. Boys were superior to girls in every department and most of us couldn’t see what use they were.

The two girls grinned at one another. “Ah but rules are meant to be broken aren’t they?”

“Not this one,” said Davie firmly, and we all agreed. Girls even in this clearing had never happened before, so there was no way they would be allowed to enter our secret hideout.

“Alright,” said the cheeky Angela. “Don’t get your pants in a twist we don’t need to come inside your silly old hut anyway.”

The reference to our pants was embarrassing enough, coming as it did from two girls. But to refer to the headquarters of the Sundance gang as our silly old hut was nothing short of insulting. We did at least hear them out, and what they had to say made sense.

“Look,” Angela said. “It will take at least ten of us to sew that big piece of cloth into something that will do as a sail.

There are enough of us in our class to do that. It will be properly done and will take that raft of yours down the Gest to Westbridge Docks faster than you could imagine. But there are other things we can do. You'll need stores, sandwiches, cakes, that sort of thing. We can arrange that for you, and we're all prepared to help you in your fight with the boys from Brimly village."

"How can you do that?" we asked.

Fighting the Brimly's was boys work, and as I had already said to my dad, it was our fight and ours alone. We certainly wouldn't have girls anywhere around when it came to clashing with them.

"We don't mean actually fighting. We can help in other ways."

"How?" demanded an impatient Davie.

Every time we had a score to settle with Frank Thornton's gang, and we had been at odds with them for a long time, it was us boys who took up the challenge. And in fairness to the Brimlys it was always just the nine of them we had to contend with. Or so we had always thought.

"How do you think the Brimly boys always know what you lot are doing?" Frances asked.

"We don't know, but we think they must keep watch from over their side of the river."

"You're nearly right, but it's not the boys who do that, it's the girls."

"What do you mean the girls? We don't have anything to do with them."

"Maybe not," said Frances, "but they have a lot to do with you. We play them at netball, so we know them as well as you know the boys. We can tell you that their netball captain Denise Keppel is every bit as crafty as the leader of the boys

Frank Thornton. She leads the girls of Brimly and she's helped by her two best friends, Alice Truelove and Glenda Pringle. We know they go to Denise's house where they can see right across the river to this clearing, through a telescope in her bedroom window. They know everything you are doing because they watch you doing it. Then of course they tell Frank Thornton."

"How do you know this?" I asked.

"I told you," said Angela. "We know them and they know us. We know what they get up to and it's only boys who think girls are soft. Denise Keppel likes Frank Thornton a lot and he's too stupid to even realize it. But he does take notice of everything she tells him. Especially if it helps his gang put one over on you."

"So how can you help us to hit back at them?" asked Davie.

"By doing much the same as they do," said Angela. "We can make the sail in the shed at my house, and bring it here when it's ready to go on the raft. Then when you start off, Frances and I, along with at least eight more girls from our class will be stationed along the banks of the river. If any of us see anything that will threaten your trip and your raft, we will get a warning to you in time for you to take preventative action."

"This sounds very good to me," said Davie. "But why do you and the rest of the girls want to do this for us?"

"Because you're our boys and because we owe the Brimly girls revenge for the way they've treated us so many times."

So we left it there with an agreement in place for our girls to be involved in the great Kon Tiki challenge. We were sure it would be triumphant this time around.

With harvest now safely over and everything gathered in, it was time for the local farmers to prepare the fields for sowing next year's crop. The fertilizer, made up mainly of dung from the cattle, was put into muck spreading vehicles which were driven over the fields, spraying out this awful smelling stuff as they went.

At this time of year it was necessary to hold your breath for long periods of time, because of the terrible stink this created. No matter how long anyone had lived in this vicinity, when muck spreading was taking place windows were always firmly closed. Even we avoided the fields at this time. But the dreadful pong still found us at our headquarters. It seemed inevitable that yet another highly embarrassing moment was about to overtake us.

It all happened so quickly. We were on our way home when one of the local farm hands came up behind us. He had been out all day spraying the fields, and was looking forward to getting back to the farm for a well deserved tea. He saw us walking along and shouted over, "want a lift lads?"

It was all so innocent. A lift home was a lift home, and what did it matter if it was on a muck spreader. We jumped at the chance and piled on, Phil Landers riding up front alongside the driver, while the rest of us clung on where we could.

And that was the problem. Phil was the sort of boy who always had to know how things worked. Many times when he had been given clockwork toys for his birthday and at Christmas, he was never happy until he knew what made them go. To find out he took them apart, which was fine up to a point. But he always found that having taken them to pieces he could never put them back together again. His father spent many hours doing this for him, and trying to get him not to do it again. He would also push a button or pull a lever just to see what would happen.

Today, as he sat on the muck spreader, he noticed a lever down by his feet. Without a thought about the consequences he asked "what does this do?" at the same time pulling on the lever.

The driver shouted at him in alarm. "Don't touch it."

It was too late.

The lever started the mechanism that sprayed the awful fertilizer. We were not in the fields though and had reached the main village street. Before the spraying could be stopped, one of the shops was now covered in this evil smelling brown mess.

The one in question was owned and run by a lady from London, Miss Alice Ellerington, and was a very posh place. This was a disaster. Miss Ellerington had arrived in Surlington during the last war. She came to escape the constant bombing in London and liked the village so much she bought the property she now owned and opened her shop. 'Ladies Gowns of Distinction' was the name of it, and she sold expensive ladies dresses.

I had often heard my mum talking about this shop with the other women of the village. None of them bought anything here because, as mum said, "everything in there is too expensive." She bought most of her clothes from a catalogue and paid for them on a weekly basis. She also went into Westbridge at least once a month and bought things like hats and shoes. Miss Ellerington's customers were the same ones who had frequented her London store and came down to our village to buy these posh dresses from here. Now this elegant establishment looked nothing like a place of distinction.

The lady in question stumbled out holding a big handkerchief over her nose and mouth and started shouting at us all.

“Look at my beautiful store,” she wailed. “I’m ruined. My ladies will not come anymore to buy my lovely gowns. What a smell.”

With this she disappeared back inside.

There was a predictable outcry about what had happened. All of the adults of the village came running to see what the commotion was about and all gagged at the awful smell. Coming as it did from the front of this previously elegant ladies gown shop. My parents both came out from the Dog and Duck, leaving the bars in the care of Mavis our barmaid. While dad started to weigh up the situation outside, my mum with two of the other ladies went inside to see what they could do for Miss Ellerington.

Mum was the best person to do this because she was more used to dealing with people who were in any sort of trouble. Many times, since she and dad had been landlord and landlady of our pub, she had listened to tales of woe from one customer or another. She usually managed to give the right advice, or comfort, if this was all that was needed to fit the situation. This though was a huge challenge, even for her. Miss Ellerington was as posh as her shop and was now screaming to sue the person responsible for such cruel and wanton damage to her lovely premises.

My mum went swiftly into ‘operation sooth’ and sent the other two ladies to make tea and bring a cup, with plenty of sugar in, as soon as they could. She then spoke very calmly to this distressed lady and said that what had happened was an accident. No-one in this village, or any other for that matter, would do something like this on purpose.

"But my store," wailed the lady. "I am ruined, ruined I tell you."

"Nonsense," said mum. "Most of the village men, and some from the farms are outside now, and I can assure you they will put things right for you. They will have this store cleaned up and ready for business tomorrow morning, if they have to work all night to do it."

She said this in a very determined voice, so determined it got through, even to Miss Ellerington. Mum neither knew, nor particularly liked this woman. Not only were her gowns too expensive for the village ladies, but when her customers came down from London she was in the habit of entertaining them to an evening of cocktails. For this she went to the other pub in our village the White Swan, never to the Dog and Duck.

She also failed to use any of the village stores for her needs, everything she wanted was ordered by telephone and delivered to her store. Many times we had heard our own parents, and other villagers, complaining that she thought none of us were good enough for her, which made this present situation even worse.

Outside my father was saying just that as he tried to find out how this could possibly have happened. The now thoroughly worried farm hand who had been driving the spreader was trying to explain.

"I shouted to the nipper not to pull the lever," he told dad. "But it was too late, he'd already pulled the bloody thing, and look at the result. This will cost me my job when Mr Davidson sees it."

"Don't worry about Ted Davidson," dad told him. "He and I grew up together. We'll work this out between us. Just don't tell him you gave these boys a lift."

To us as well this warning was very firmly given. "None of you were on this spreader when this happened. You were just walking past, got it?"

When dad spoke as firmly as that, and glared as he said it, we all knew this was no time to argue. We therefore nodded in agreement. To the farm hand he said, "Now listen, Ted's running down the lane and will be here in a matter of minutes. Those boys were never on that muck spreader, you were driving back to the farm when your knee accidently hit the lever and started the spreading mechanism."

The farm hand agreed quickly enough, he would have said anything to get out of this horrible situation. Because while it was true he didn't set it off, he knew he shouldn't have given us a lift on it. Ted Davidson, who owned Brook farm, came running up and stopped in stupefied amazement at the mess his spreader had done to the front of this shop. He turned on the farm hand and shouted at him to explain himself. The poor man repeated what my father had told him to say, but his boss was far from satisfied.

"How can you accidently shift the lever? You know what will happen if you do, this," he said pointing at the shop, now oozing evil smelling dung down the front, covering the door and both of the large windows.

"Ok Ted, you're obviously angry and rightly so," dad said to him. "But right now we need to do something about this."

"I'm not only angry," Mr Davidson replied. "I'm bloody worried. She could sue me over this and if she does she can ruin me."

"All the more reason we act quickly then," dad told him. The farm hand was ordered straight away to drive the muck spreader back to the farm, and to stay there out of sight.

Then all of the men began work to restore Miss Ellerington's exclusive gown shop to its former glory. This was done with a big wash down, using stiff yard brooms. Our job being to carry buckets of soapy water, and disinfectant to make sure this work went on without a hitch. All of us, both men and boys, wore handkerchiefs over our faces to ward off the smell. Phil Landers kept very much to himself because he knew that with us at least, he wasn't exactly popular at the moment.

While we were working our socks off outside, my mum and the other ladies had moved the dummies from the window and brought them out to the back of the shop. This was so the smell from outside would not get into the cloth of the expensive dresses that were displayed on them. We were sent home to bed at nine o'clock, but the men went on working and by morning when I was up and on my way to school with the others, Miss Ellerington's shop looked clean and elegant again. There was now no sign of the mess that had been all over it last night, or the terrible smell.

While I was eating my breakfast mum told me that they were up until the small hours of the morning. The men cleaning and painting some parts of the shop front to bring it back to its usual posh look. The woman had stayed with Miss Ellerington until the big clean up was finished and had then led her outside to see the result.

"Oh," she had said, "it looks wonderful now you would never have thought anything had happened at all, thank you so much everyone."

To have this lady thanking them all was something none of them had expected and everyone was pleased, even Mr Davidson. After apologising to her they came to an agreement about the situation. He accepted responsibility for the accident because it was his muck spreader that had caused it. But because it was an accident Miss Ellerington accepted his offer of free dairy produce for the next three months, so honour was satisfied all round. What happened to the farm hand that had been driving the muck spreader we never found out, but none of us saw him again after that day.

At school we made poor Phil's life a misery. Every time one of us was close to him we whispered, "What does this lever do?" He got fed up with it of course.

When Paul Edwards did it Phil had taken enough and he lashed out. The result was a fight which brought every boy running up to watch. This was broken up very quickly by Mr Bond who was on playground duty. Both Phil and Paul were hauled up before Miss Tuttle who said this sort of behaviour was not welcome in her school. They both got six strokes of the cane, three on each hand. When they came back out, both blowing on their hands to ease the stinging, they were friends again. This was a relief because we had to discuss getting even with our real enemies, the boys in the Brimly gang.

In the hideout that weekend Davie looked at us all from his lofty perch, as he always did.

"Boys I have one thing to say to you and that is pooh."

We just sat and looked at him. What on earth was he talking about?

"Yes I know you think I've gone daft, but not so. This is how we are going to avenge the wrecking of our raft and the theft of the Colonel's apple. And don't any of you forget it was them that told on us and got us in so much trouble over it."

He needn't have worried about that, we were still smarting over all of the things he had just outlined.

"But how are we going to do it?" I asked. "Why pooh?"

“Stink bombs,” said Davie. “That’s what we’re going to use against them.”

Stink bombs had already caused us a certain amount of trouble earlier in the year. Keith Andrews had an uncle who owned a joke shop and always knew what was coming out in this line. He had buttonhole flowers that squirted water at people, whoopee cushions that made a rude noise whenever anyone sat on them, and all manner of things designed to make people look fools and give the perpetrators a good laugh. So it wasn’t any surprise to us when he turned up at our headquarters one day with a box of little glass tubes.

“What are these”? Davie had asked him.

“They’ve come in to my uncle’s shop,” said Keith, “they’re stink bombs.”

I laughed to myself now as I remembered Davie picking one up and holding it to his nose.

“I can’t smell anything.”

“That’s because the glass hasn’t broken,” Keith told him. “If it had you would have known all about it. My uncle said the stink is awful once the glass breaks.”

He then made the mistake of bringing some to school. During the arithmetic lesson in the morning he whispered to Davie that one of the bombs was missing.

“What do you mean missing?” hissed back Davie.

“I had two of them when I came into class, now I can only find one.”

Miss Tuttle had set us a maths problem and walked silently around the classroom as we tried to work out the answer. There was just the tiniest of tinkling sounds as her foot landed on top of the stink bomb that Keith had accidentally dropped on the floor.

In just a few seconds we found out why these things were so called. The awful pong that filled that classroom had the effect of clearing the room in record time. All of us, Miss Tuttle included, rushed out to the fresh air of the playground. It took over half an hour for the stench to clear from the room so we could all go back inside.

Needless to say there was a very big hoo haa about this and if we had given Keith away he would have been in very big trouble indeed. We didn't of course, he was in our gang, and all of us were still laughing about the incident for a long time afterwards. Now Davie was saying we would use these against the Brimly's, but how?

"I've been talking to Angela," he said, "and she's told me that our school has been drawn to play Brimly in the next round of the inner schools netball championship."

This statement was met by eight blank stares that suggested so what? None of us had the least interest in this girl's game, so why was Davie telling us about it?

"I know," he said. "None of you are interested in netball. Nor am I, but this is a cup match and I know Miss Tuttle is keen for our girls to win it. So keen in fact that she is organising a coach to take as many of us from our school over there to support our girls. Now, as you know, Brimly have their carnival late in the year and Frank Thornton and the rest of them will all be up on their float. The girls have found out it's decorated as a pirate ship and they will be dressed as pirates.

At the back of the float, which I believe is mounted on one of the local farmers lorries, will be the Carnival Queen. This year that will be Denise Keppel and she will have two maids of honour sitting on either side of her, Alice Truelove on one side and Glenda Pringle on the other. We owe these three girls in particular because we know it was them who gave away the news of our raft to the Brimly boys, and that's how they were able to plan the destruction of it. We will therefore put our names down to go on the coach to their school and while the game is being played we'll sneak away."

"Keith," he asked, "how many of those stink bombs have you got left?"

"Fifteen," he replied. "There were sixteen originally, but as you know I dropped one in class and Miss Tuttle trod on it."

"That's ok," said Davie. "Fifteen will be more than enough."

"What have you got in mind Davie?" I asked.

"Well if everything goes to plan we'll go on this coach. It will take us around the long route then over the bridge across the river before we arrive at their school. We'll wait until the game is well under way then, one at a time, we'll all drift off. The float is in their playground, so all we need to do is position our stink bombs in places where they will either be stepped on or sat on. The stink will be terrific, and they'll have to put up with it because the procession will already be moving. Their float in particular has to be seen by everyone especially as it has the Carnival Queen aboard."

"It sounds good Davie," said Mickie Tranter. "But will we get away with it?

"Why shouldn't we?" asked Davie.

"Well just think about it," went on Mickie. "If this game was being played at our school and Frank Thornton and his lot came to watch it, we would be watching them all the time to make sure they didn't do anything to us at our school."

"Yes I realise that, but the beauty of this is that netball is a sissy girl's game, and that means the Brimly boys won't come anywhere near it."

We all saw the wisdom of this, because watching girls play netball was not high on our list of interesting things to do either. Miss Trout, who was in charge of the girl's team, and also in charge of the coach to get us all to the match, was not just surprised, but flabbergasted when we asked for our names to be included.

"Well you're certainly all welcome," she said. "But where has this sudden interest in the game of netball come from?"

"We've been talking to some of the girls about it," said Davie, "and according to them this should be a good game to watch besides we always want to cheer on Surlington when we're against Brimly."

Miss Trout smiled at this then said "Alright you're all welcome to come, but remember this is a sport, and the game will be played in a sporting manner. It's not simply a contest to see who are better between the two villages."

"Of course Miss," we all agreed, and with a look of, 'I don't really trust you lot', she none-the-less put our names on her list.

So on Friday we turned up outside our playground and boarded the netball coach. Our girls knew why we were going but no one else did which was why we got some very funny looks from the others who were genuine netball followers. We enjoyed the short trip across the river but as Brimly came into sight all of us grew tense. This might be a quaint little English village, but it was the home of our sworn enemies.

We followed everyone else around the back of Brimly school to the playing fields, and there started to watch the cup tie between their girls and ours. How anyone can watch a game like this will always be beyond me. The girls of both teams had jerseys on with initials on the front. Some had GK while others had GS, WD etc. The first thing I noticed was that they had two referees, one in each half of the field. Why was that I wondered, couldn't these older women run fast enough to keep up with the play? And that wasn't exactly a difficult thing to do either. The girls hardly seemed to be moving.

I watched as the ball flew through the air straight into the arms of Angela Ford. Even from where I was standing I could see she had a clear run into the other half of the field, and a good chance to score. Instead she stopped and looked around before throwing the ball on to Michelle Anton. I couldn't believe it. Why stop like that when you could run on and dump the ball through the hoop for a goal? It wasn't just Angela who did this but all of the girls from both teams. I was reaching the bored out of my skull stage when Davie hissed in my ear.

"Billy, come on we're moving." He didn't have to tell me twice, anything would be better than standing here watching this.

All nine of us approached the playground of the enemy from different directions. Once there we climbed up onto their pirate float.

"Here they are," said Keith, producing a bulky bag from under his pullover.

"Right now let's do this right," said Davie. At the far end was a raised platform with a decorated chair, this was the throne of the Carnival Queen. There were two stools on either side for the maids of honour.

The rest of the float was very well set out. It really did look like the deck of a pirate ship. A lot of work had obviously gone into this and for a few minutes I had doubts about what we were planning to do. Davie however reminded me of all the effort we had made to build the raft that this lot wrecked.

After that I joined in with gusto and between us all of our stink bombs were placed around the float. Three under the seats the girls would sit on, and twelve that with a bit of luck would be trodden on by the Brimly boys.

We rejoined the netball match and found that our girls had won by a big margin. So the whole trip had been a success as far as we were concerned. On the way back the girls, all happy because they beaten their bitter rivals, asked us what we thought of the game. We should have bluffed it out and told them we enjoyed it very much.

But no, all of us, especially me, spoke out about how boring and what a waste of time a game like netball was.

"What do you mean by that?" asked Angela. She knew we weren't there to watch the match, but wasn't too pleased to hear us being so negative about netball in general. She, like the rest of the girls, enjoyed the game and was good at it. So the criticism from us was not being received very well. We weren't worried though because of course we were right. What do girls know about ball games anyway?

Finding the whole thing immensely funny we were suddenly confronted by Miss Trout. She had been alerted to this situation by one of the girls and had heard most of what we were saying about a game she was passionate about and loomed over us.

"I thought there was something fishy about you wanting to come and support us at this game. Now I don't know what you're up to but I can be pretty certain it's nothing to do with sport. So I will be keeping a very special eye on all of you over the next few days. As for your comments about the game of netball, well we'll have to see what we can do about that. Wont we?"

This was a new side to Miss Trout that none of us had seen before. She took our whole class for some lessons, but it was girls she took for sports and PT. The only thing I had enjoyed about the part of the netball match I had seen was the sight of her in the tight top and shorts she always wore. It was still disturbing me. This outburst, and the way she was glaring at us was something new and faintly worrying. In just two weeks time we would find out how much.

Chapter 7

Upon returning to school we hurried into Banter wood to discuss our plans for tomorrow. Davie had told Angela we would include them in anything we did because she and the other girls had helped set up what should be a wonderful revenge on the Brimly gang. I had already spoken to my dad about what we were going to do. After outlining the plan he had given it some thought.

"Ok Billy, there may be a row about this afterwards. Still, we'll take care of that, if and when it happens."

He was laughing as he walked away, then turned and added, "Billy remember what I told you, don't get caught."

We had been speaking with Commander Phillips a lot recently and heard wonderful stories of the Navy under sail in the days of Lord Nelson. In battles with enemy ships marksmen would be stationed aloft. From here they could fire muskets down onto the decks of the enemy, usually aiming for the officers. Davie had decided this tactic would also work for us.

Just down from our clearing, and adjacent to Brimly High Street on the other side of the river, were some of the tallest oak trees along the banks of the Gest. Climbing into the branches of these we would be able to see if our stink bomb ploy had worked. We could also make things even more difficult for them on that float by using catapults.

We were all very good with these. Even our newest member David Callow had shown that boy scouts have a very good aim with this extremely useful weapon. Until now we had used them to take pot shots at targets we set up in the woods, and of course fired at each other when we were playing. Now though, to put this latest plan into operation we needed much bigger and more powerful catapults. We would be firing across to the other side of the river, which at that particular point was at one of its widest stretches. So to achieve this we would need stronger and stouter sticks, and the secret weapon, strong elastic.

This we obtained from a little shop at the far end of Surlington High Street. It was run by a very old lady Miss Lillian Philpot. Our mother's could buy things for making and mending everything in our homes from her. Wool for knitting, cotton for sewing, needles and pins were all available here. They could also get elastic in varying strengths from this shop. When my mum needed what she called, strong knicker elastic, she always said, "I need to go to Lillies." So that's where we went as well.

Miss Philpot looked over her counter at us when we asked for quite a lot of this strong elastic, and asked what we wanted it for. We blushed deep red when she said, "I don't think you want it for keeping your knickers up do you?" We hastily assured her this was not our purpose and Davie went on to explain that we wanted it for our new catapults. She just grinned at us and said "Well that's more like it boys, how much do you need?"

Now we were ready and early the next day, which was the Saturday of the Brimly Carnival, we were all in position in the trees. The girls had surprised us that morning by turning up in the woods prepared for climbing. They were all wearing their oldest clothes and wanted to see what was going on across the river. We all knew of course girls can't climb and Davie pointed this out to them. Angela and the rest were ready for this so she looked round.

“Right girls, let’s show this lot.”

With that they all ran at the nearest tree and started to climb up into the branches. Twelve girls were there that morning and every one of them was aloft in the trees before us. We couldn’t believe what we were seeing, girls are useless at climbing, at least that’s what we had always thought, but they had shown us this wasn’t true at all.

It was not a good start and we were determined to regain our stature as soon as possible. Once into the trees we could see right into the Brimly school’s playground. The far end of their high street was clearly visible so we would know what was going on as they approached the rest of the procession. Denise Keppel stood on the float and as it left the school playground she moved to the far end where her throne was, ready to sit in splendour and wave to the crowd as they went past. Her two maids of honour, Glenda Truelove and Alice Pringle were there beside her.

The float rounded the corner at the top of the high street and the girls took their places. Denise sat down and regally waved as the float moved slowly and sedately along. As we watched however her face suddenly changed and a look of absolute horror passed over it. She gagged and placed her hands across her nose, the two girls on either side had already done this and we were over the moon. The first three stink bombs had been set off and there were twelve more to go.

Frank Thornton had noticed that all was not well with the girls and started to move forward to find what was wrong. Suddenly stopping as he stepped on one of the bombs, he turned to shout a warning to the others not to move, but it was too late. They had come forward and also stepped on the stink bombs.

Now they all had to stay on their pirate float and travel the whole distance around their village with this awful smell filling the air around them. They knew at once of course that we were responsible for this and all the boys glared across to our side of the river.

That was what we had been waiting for and Davie shouted, "Now."

All nine of us let fly with our new catapults and fired round after round of conkers across the river. This caused even more confusion on the Brimly float as everyone on it dived for cover. We kept up this bombardment until they were out of range.

Every one of us enjoyed this so much even the girls were laughing themselves silly.

"Did you see Denise Keppel's face?" said Angela, between bouts of laughter.

The other girls nodded, they had enjoyed the Brimly girls downfall, as much as we had enjoyed getting one back on the boys. Victory to the Sundance gang was the shout as we made our way to headquarters with the girls going back to the village.

We spent the rest of that weekend in our domain in Banter Wood doing all the things we loved to do. Climbing, swimming and chasing each other around without a care in the world. The trouble started when we went back to school on Monday. Mr Leigh, a big man who taught PT and Sports at Brimly school was in Miss Tuttle's study. Unknown to us he had come to complain about the atrocious behaviour of some of her pupils, namely us.

Miss Tuttle looked at him and said quietly, "And which pupils are we talking about Mr Leigh?"

"I have a list here. The names of the boys involved," he said, handing our headmistress a piece of paper with all our names written on it.

"Yes," she said. "These boys do attend this school, but I understand the incident you are complaining about, happened on a Saturday."

"That's right," said the agitated Mr Leigh. "The day of the Brimly Carnival and may I add, this is something that has taken place in our village for more years than I can remember. This year, thanks to these hooligans, the whole thing was ruined."

"Well Mr Leigh, first of all I must point out that Saturday is not a school day, so what these boys do with their time when they are not in school is nothing to do with us. Furthermore can you positively tell me these are the boys who, as you say ruined your carnival?"

"Our pupils who were on our school float have no doubts on that score Madam," he said. "You are correct that the act of sabotage, namely conkers being fired across the river, was done on a Saturday. But this was set up by these boys when they came to Brimly school on Friday evening pretending to support your girl's netball team. They positioned these evil smelling stink bombs around our float, in places where it was more than likely they would be trodden on. We found evidence of ten of these which were broken and three that weren't.

Our boys had to spend nearly all of Sunday cleaning the lorry bed that our float was on. The farmer who owns it was not at all pleased when he got a whiff of the stench. He uses it to deliver vegetables to local traders, and to have a smell like that clinging to his lorry would do his business no good at all. The whole carnival was ruined by this. When the crowd that were watching came into reach of our pirate float, they had to reel back because of the horrible smell. It got into our children's clothes, and their parents are now complaining. Things like trousers, jumpers, shirts, and in the girl's cases, skirts as well had to be thrown away."

Mr Leigh ran out of breath at that point and Miss Tuttle took advantage of the pause to speak quietly.

"I am distressed to hear of the consequences and I certainly will be speaking to the boys concerned to hear their side of it. After that I will telephone Brimly school's headmaster Mr Watkins. Thank you for bringing this to my attention. Good morning Mr Leigh."

That afternoon all nine of us were summoned to Miss Tuttle's study. Forming a line in front of her desk we listened to the complaints, not only from Brimly school, but also the parents of Frank Thornton's gang and some of the people who lived in that village.

"I want to hear your side of this," she said. "Did you sabotage the Brimly school float by placing stink bombs on it? And did you further, on Saturday, fire conkers across the river aimed at that same float?"

We stood silently in front of her, no-one wanting to answer. It seemed such a lot of fun when we were planning and carrying this out. But now, having been read back to us like this, it somehow lost all of its humour.

"I see from the way you are all studying your shoes that the answer to my question is yes," she said.

Davie now spoke up. "Please Miss, we did do everything you've just mentioned but we had our reasons."

"I'm sure you did Davie Collins, but I will need to know what those reasons are before I can make any decision about whether to involve your parents in this."

"I'm sorry Miss, but it's between us and a gang from that school. It's a private fight and we, as well as they, want to keep it that way."

"Very well," said Miss Tuttle. "But I must warn you that you have caused a lot of trouble to the people in the village of Brimly. You can expect to hear a lot more about this."

We were then dismissed and sent back to class. For the next two days nothing happened and we were beginning to think we had got away with it. But when I came home from school on the third day after Miss Tuttle's warning, it was to find my father waiting for me.

"Right Billy," he said. "You and all the rest of your gang, as well as some of the girls, are to come to the village hall tonight. There is to be a meeting between us and Brimly about this carnival float business. Don't worry," he said as he saw the alarm, that leaped into my face. "You all had your reasons and we'll be there to speak up for you."

By seven thirty that evening Surlington village hall was filled with grownups and children from both villages. The Reverend Morley was on the raised platform at the front of the hall that served as a stage. He made a loud banging sound with a mallet then yelled for order.

"Ladies and Gentlemen," he said. "We are here this evening to discuss a grievance about an incident that took place in Brimly village last Saturday. As I understand it a carnival float was sabotaged by a group of boys from this village."

This statement was met by a roar of sound from the floor of the hall. The villagers from across the river shouting about how awful it was and how they wanted something called compensation for their children's ruined clothes. The Reverend tried to restore order but the noise got louder and louder and he had no success at all. It wasn't looking good for us and we looked at each other, wondering what was going to happen next. There was suddenly a very loud voice from beside the vicar that shouted one word, "Silence."

It stunned everyone and did indeed achieve its aim. The hall went quiet as we all looked at the person who had shouted. It was my father. Nobody, not even me, had seen him go up onto the stage. But there he stood glaring at the assembled crowd.

"I haven't heard such a load of rubbish in a very long time," he said. "This nonsense about ruined clothing, all you women have to do is soak them in sunlight soap then give them a good scrub. Even we men know that, what we have here is a case of boys being boys and you're all over reacting."

The clamour started again as the Brimly parents argued this wasn't so.

"What right do your boys think they have to ruin a lot of hard work that goes into a carnival float? They have spoilt a tradition that has gone on for over a hundred years," shouted a very large lady in the front row.

"I imagine the same right the boys from Brimly school thought they had when they sabotaged our boys raft a few weeks ago," my dad answered her.

"Only they did it in such a way that the raft would break apart in the middle of the River Gest, and dump them into the water. No-one in that reckless gang gave any thought to our boy's safety. They went into the water fully dressed and could have been dragged under as a result. They were only saved from this by the fact that all of them are good swimmers. Does that answer your question madam?" he finished.

The large lady could think of nothing to say to this so she just sat and glared. It was then that Mr Leigh, who had been to our school three days before, stood up.

"No-one from Brimly school would do anything as reckless and dangerous as that."

"Really?" my dad replied. "Then I suggest you have a word with a lad by the name of Frank Thornton, and the rest of the boys who follow him around."

Mr and Mrs Thornton now started shouting that their son would never do anything like that, and if any of us said he did then we must be wicked liars. I thought I had seen my father angry before, but now, under this insult to his son, he simply erupted.

"My son is not a liar. Madam, he is a Christian boy, taught to tell the truth. He told me about the way your son, and his daft friends, deliberately cut through the ropes holding their raft together. They watched as it came apart and laughed as our boys plunged into the water. My son and all his friends saw who was responsible because they did nothing to hide the fact. They were proud of themselves and ran along the bank of the river on your side, laughing and taunting our boys. Is it any wonder they wanted revenge?"

There was a long pause in the proceedings after that and we had the satisfaction of seeing Frank Thornton and co being grilled by their parents. In his case, when he did eventually own up to the wrecking of the raft, he got a very hard clip round his ears.

The situation had to be brought to some kind of solution though and after our parents and some of the Brimly grown-ups had conferred, my dad once again called for silence.

“Alright everyone, a lot has been said tonight about the behaviour of both sets of boys, from this village and from Brimly. One thing seems to be of top importance. They both think they have been wronged and both want revenge on each other. So we have decided to let them do this but in an organised and proper fashion. There will be a boxing match between these two groups, to be held here, in this hall, in four weeks time.”

There was a general stir of interest at this news and we started to make rude gestures to the Brimly boys, who did the same back to us. A boxing match, we couldn’t wait.

The meeting broke up after that and my dad went back to the Dog and Duck. A lot of the Brimly grownups went there also to have a drink before going home. Among these were Frank Thornton’s parents and Bill Grimes’ aunt. They came with them of course and were given lemonade to drink in the pub garden. It was weird for Davie and me to see this. These two were our sworn enemies, yet here they were in the garden of my mum and dad’s pub. We never let them out of our sight all the time they were there, and goaded them about the obvious outcome of the boxing match.

They had their own opinion of course, and the language they used telling us what was going to happen to all of our boys was shocking.

“You lot are going to look a lot different with black eyes and cut lips after the match,” Davie said.

Bill Grimes replied to this.

“Yeah, you Sundance kids ain’t got what it takes to hurt any of us. We’re gonna smash your faces.”

“Yeah and you’ll all be off school for months,” Frank said.

Davie and I just looked at each other, before lifting our fingers in a very rude sign at them both.

We met again in the village hall that weekend, to talk about the coming boxing match, and how to prepare the Sundance Gang for this encounter. We had all been involved in playground fights many times, but this was different. We would be boxing in a real ring with a referee. So my dad, again taking charge, asked for ideas.

"Well," said a very posh voice from the back of the hall. "It will all have to be done under the Queensbury rules."

This was Colonel Worthington-Pugh of course. He really did have a most peculiar way of speaking.

Prior to the last war he had spent most of his army career in India, as part of the British Raj. Whenever he wanted something done he just snapped his fingers and a servant magically appeared. I had heard one story from this period of time, told to all of us with a great amount of glee by Commander Phillips. The Colonel was in the garden of his house in Nanjapour, when he saw a poisonous snake slithering towards him. There was a pistol in a holster on his hip and a sword within easy reach, but all he did was yell for his house-boy, who happened to be a woman. When she came running he pointed to the snake and said, "Take care of that will you."

She then had to deal with this dangerous situation by herself, while he went on enjoying his evening gin and tonic. That was the life he knew before starting to earn his rank, as he did with distinction during the Second World War. His previous days in India though left him with this very affected voice. When he mentioned the Queensbury rules, it sounded as though he said the Queensbury Rooels.

"Thank you Colonel," said dad. "We all know that, but I mean who is going to train these boys to box?"

"Well I am deah boy, yes you can leave that to me," the army officer answered. He always addressed other male grownups as deah boy and us as little boys. So our training, which had to be the best we could get, would be done under the supervision of the Colonel.

We had seen a different side of him at the harvest festival choir practice. But this was important to us. Nothing less than victory would be acceptable in any sort of conflict with the boys of Brimly village. We were saved by the interruption of Commander Phillips.

"Good for you Colonel and I'll help you."

He was not happy with this and said so straight away. "Thank you deah boy, but that won't be necessary."

"Oh I think it will," said the Commander. "As you may recall Colonel, I was once the boxing champion aboard the Battle Cruiser HMS Vanguard. And to achieve that I had to be able to box, because there were some very big men aboard that wanted to prove they were the best. The fact I beat most of them to win the championship gives me good enough credentials to assist you in preparing these boys for this match."

The Colonel spluttered a bit but could find no reason to refuse his next door neighbours offer.

Training began the next night and we all turned up on time at the village hall. The Colonel talked to us first, telling us that the honour of the village was at stake. We knew that of course, and it wasn't only the village's honour either. Defeat at this match would have very serious consequences for our gang. So it was victory or bust for us. When it was my turn to put on the gloves, I entered the ring and prepared to square up to big Tommy Stack. He worked at the village butcher shop and had agreed to act as sparring partner for all of us. I put up my guard and faced this bigger boy in the centre of the ring.

Before anything started however the Colonel's loud voice interrupted.

"What do you think you're doing little boy?" he roared. "You're the wrong way round."

I had suffered this at school whenever we faced each other in a boxing ring. Each time my stance was challenged. As I put up my dukes I always naturally led with my right, keeping the left tucked under my chin, ready to hit when I got the chance. Unfortunately for me, this was considered to be wrong. Everyone was supposed to lead with their left and hit with their right. To me this wasn't natural, and I couldn't do it. The normally calm Colonel was starting to get very angry indeed but it was the Commander who sorted it out.

"Just a minute Colonel," he said. "I remember a stoker on the Vanguard who fought like this. Some people, like little Billy here, can't fight any other way. It's not as though they're left handed or anything. They just lead with their right instead of doing it the recognised way. These fighters are becoming known as south paws. I had quite a difficult job fighting against this man because he was coming at me the wrong way. But I worked it out and managed to beat him."

"So Billy," he said, ruffling my hair. "You do it your way and we'll support you."

As I prepared to start boxing Tommy Stack, the Commander said, "Your best defence against a boy of this size is to make sure he doesn't get the chance to hit you."

Dad had said the same thing to me as we boxed each other in the kitchen of the Dog and Duck.

"Use your speed and agility Billy. Keep out of your opponents reach and make him miss every time he tries to hit you. You'll wear him out and get to land a few punches of your own."

The Commander was now telling me the same thing. "Keep bouncing on your feet Billy, use your speed and attack him when you get the chance."

This was good advice, but not the easiest thing to put into practice. I boxed three rounds against Tommy that day and was well and truly out of it by the end. I hadn't kept out of his way and as a result got floored in every round. Both the Colonel and the Commander made sympathetic noises as I groggily made my way back to the little room we were using for changing. The rest of the gang rallied round me and Davie in particular gave me so much encouragement.

"Don't worry Billy," he said, "by the time we meet that lot from Brimly we'll have you dancing around the ring."

To achieve this he brought in Angela and the girls.

"You need to learn how to skip Billy," she told me. "Then you can keep out of trouble when you're boxing."

So for the next four days I was put through endless skipping lessons from the girls, and slowly began to get the hang of it. My ring performances were improving and as a result I actually managed to land a corker of a right hand punch on Tommy Stack's jaw that had him reeling back against the ropes. The great haw haw haw of the Colonel rang out at this and he bellowed, "Well done that little boy."

The Commander just winked at me and then mouthed, "I told you so."

I went to bed that night very happy indeed, I told dad how successful I had been today and he was delighted. My mum didn't share his enthusiasm. She wasn't happy about her son fighting in a boxing match and had given dad a hard time over it.

"If he gets hurt," she raged at him one night, "it will be your fault."

“He won’t get hurt,” dad argued. “Good heavens dear he’s a boy, and boys get into fights, that’s the way it is.”

It went on like this right up until the night of the match. Both my parents were there, having made sure the Dog and Duck was in good hands. I was down to fight second and was drawn against David Conner. I didn’t know a lot about him but knew that he was bigger than me, both taller and stronger. So it was not going to be an easy fight.

In the ring first was Johnnie White for us and John Kingsley for Brimly. This started well, Johnnie was a boy who knew how to look after himself, and he won the first two of the three scheduled rounds. Unfortunately, both for him and us, John Kingsley caught Johnnie with a punch that landed above his right eye causing a cut.

Colonel Worthington-Pugh was refereeing and immediately stepped in. One look was enough and he stopped the fight in favour of Brimly. So as I climbed up into the ring we were one down, and over in the other corner was David Conner. I glanced down at my dad and he gave me the thumbs up sign, my mum just looked worried.

As the bell sounded I came out to meet my opponent and he rushed out at me. The skipping lessons really paid off. Time and time again I skipped out of range as he tried to land punches on me, and even got the chance to hit him a few times myself. My stance was confusing him too and this also helped me.

For two rounds I stayed out of his way and I could see he was tiring. Every time he swung at me and missed I could hear the breath hissing out of his body. In the second minute of the third round he swung at me and missed again. As he did this I swung my trusty left hand and connected squarely with his jaw. I jumped back in some shock. The force of that punch had shaken me as it landed. I watched in amazement as he rocked backwards and went down on his knees.

Commander Phillips was the referee for this match and he started counting. He got to eight before David Connor started to rise and reached ten before he made it. I was in a dream as the Commander raised my right arm aloft. I had won and my dad was on his feet cheering me. My mum still wasn't looking.

I was rapturously welcomed back into our dressing room and even the injured Johnnie White, a plaster now covering his right eyebrow gave me a huge hug. Davie was so pleased he wrapped both his arms around me and lifted me right off the floor.

"Well done Billy you little beauty," he shouted in my ear.

The next two fights were even. Keith Andrews easily out pointed Michael Albright, then Bob Yates was given the verdict, amid loud protests, against a very game performance from little Mickie Tranter. The evening started to go wrong for us from there. The next two fights which paired Phil Landers with Peter Warnley and Danny Meadows with Eddie Compton both ended with points verdicts that went to the Brimly team.

Davie was very worried indeed. There were three fights to go and Brimly were leading us by four wins to two. We couldn't afford to lose another one because if we did we would lose the match. Davie walked to the ring alongside Paul Edwards, urgently speaking to him and telling him the importance of his fight, he mustn't lose it. He didn't, and fought a blistering battle against Joe Lancaster. When his hand was raised at the end of it Surlington village hall erupted.

This brought our new member David Callow into the fray. David had the unenviable task of taking on the roughest member of the Brimly gang, Bill Grimes. This turned out to be three rounds of brawn against boxing skill. David had been taught to box in the scouts and had even, for a spell, been a member of a boxing club in Westbridge. Bill Grimes was king of the playground and used his superior strength to win any fight he got into. So he rushed at David from the first bell and tried to rough him up as much as he could before landing a big punch that would undoubtedly win the fight for him if it happened.

It didn't, because each time he rushed at him David simply danced out of the way, often catching Bill with counter punches and these started to make their mark. In the third round David opened up with some attacks of his own that caught his opponent completely by surprise. We cheered ourselves hoarse as the king of the Brimly playground was pounded by a succession of skilful punches that had him pinned against the ropes for most of the round.

At the final whistle Mr Leigh from Brimly, who had refereed this match, had no hesitation in raising David's hand aloft. The noise in the hall was now deafening, we had drawn level and there was only one fight left.

All of us were now convinced the match was ours because fighting last for us was our tough blacksmith's son Davie Collins. He would be up against an equally tough opponent though in the leader of the Brimly gang Frank Thornton. Frank wasn't a big lad. He was simply average in height and weight but to be gang leader he had to be able to look after himself, especially with boys like Bill Grimes in the gang.

Both of them as they entered the ring knew the honour, not only of their respective gangs but also their school and village, was now resting on their shoulders. Davie looked around the hall, at his parents sitting in the front row, at all of us, and then at the shouting and cheering girls of Surlington.

The fight started with both boys cautiously probing each other's strengths. Neither one wanted to commit themselves too early. This went on in the second round as well and even prompted Colonel Worthington-Pugh to bring them together, where they were clearly told to produce more action. At the end of the round there was nothing between them and no-one watching had any idea who was winning.

The third and final round was something I won't forget for a very long time. They walked from their corners and stood together in the centre of the ring. A strange silence descended as they stood staring at one another, then after touching gloves they both broke apart. For the next three minutes both boys stood toe to toe and threw everything they had at each other. In a flurry of punches they landed and received hits on each other. Both took no notice of these but went on handing out punishment to the other boy. At the final bell, it took the Colonel, Commander Phillips and Mr Leigh to pull them apart.

When they eventually got back in their own corners a conference was taking place outside the ring. The Colonel, the Commander, Mr Leigh and Mr Watkins, headmaster of Brimly school, talked earnestly together. This seemed to go on forever and we were beside ourselves with worry, who had won?

Finally it was Mr Watkins who entered the ring and called Davie and Frank together. They came and stood on either side of him as he raised his voice.

"Ladies and Gentlemen, in view of the remarkable round of boxing we have just witnessed, my colleagues and I cannot separate either of these two boys. Therefore the result of this contest is a draw."

He raised both Davie and Frank's right arms aloft and the cheering was so loud we couldn't hear ourselves speak. The contest as well as the match was a draw, so honour in both camps was satisfied. The thing I remember most was that even with all this noise going on, Davie from his side of the ring and Frank Thornton from his looked at each other. They didn't smile or make threatening gestures but just nodded. It was a simple nod that said so much. They were acknowledging each other and saying well done. It was the first time that any sort of truce was showing in either camp.

This lasted for the rest of the evening as the ring was packed away and a band started playing. There were drinks for the grownups from the Dog and Duck and lemonade and cakes for all of us. We enjoyed this bounty so much as we all mingled together, both the Brimly gang and the Sundance boys enjoying themselves in the same room. Our girls and theirs were also present and tried to get us up dancing, but to no avail. Not one of the boys there that night had any idea how to dance so we got out of it any way we could. Angela Ford and Denise Keppel vowed to have something done about that soon.

It was a very successful evening all round, and as the coaches taking the Brimly contingent home pulled away we waved them all off. We had enjoyed the company of Frank's boys tonight, and we almost became friends, but not quite. We still had our raft trip to go, and battle would recommence as soon as that happened.

Chapter 8

We went back to school on Monday sporting various bruises but received congratulations from our fellow pupils. Miss Tuttle said at morning assembly how proud she was of all of us and we glowed at this. Johnnie White, Phil Landers, Mickie Tranter and Danny Meadows had been down in the dumps after losing their contests. All four of them had done their best though and put up very good fights so we didn't want them feeling bad.

In class that morning Miss Trout announced that while she was proud of the way we had fought for our gang and our school, she was not pleased that we had used the netball match as a means of getting into the Brimly school playground. Nor was she amused at our assessment of this very skilful game. We couldn't help it. The mention of the word skilful along with this silly game just made us laugh. Miss Trout was not happy and promised us we would be hearing more very soon. This mild threat really meant nothing to us. Watching her glaring though, I had a funny feeling inside me.

It was a glorious week basking in the hero worship of most of the younger pupils. To draw with Brimly and satisfy our school's reputation had given us a lot of playground cred. We had given up the raft trip because of the training that was being given for the boxing. So now, nearly into October, it would have to be sooner rather than later. The weather was getting colder all the time as autumn approached, and already the leaves on the trees in Banter Wood were changing colour before dropping off altogether. Before we could finalise our plans however, Miss Trout came up with a challenge that we had little choice but to accept.

"All of you boys," she said looking straight at us, "have said a lot of nasty things lately about the game of netball. Very well, the girls and I have talked about this and are now offering you a challenge. We will play you at netball and if you beat our team, which you seem to think will be easy for you, then the girls will act as your servants for a week. However," she went on as we laughed out loud at this idea, "Should you lose the match, you will all join Miss Plumpton's ballroom dance studio and learn how to dance properly."

"Easy," we chanted and Miss Trout said she would take that as acceptance on our part. We weren't alarmed about the outcome of this, girls were no good at ball games, and playing against a team of boys gave them no chance at all. Even the daunting prospect of having to join dancing classes held no fear for us. It wasn't going to happen.

Miss Plumpton, or the widow Plumpton as our parents called her, had lived in Surlington all her life. Before any of us were even born she and her husband had owned and run the grocery store that was now in the very capable hands of Mickie Tranter's parents. Mr Plumpton had been killed in the early days of the last war. He was recalled at the start of hostilities because he was ex Navy. He had served for fifteen years in the senior service before retiring and joining his wife at the store in our village.

Unfortunately he was a crew member of the mighty Hood when she was blown up and sunk by the German battleship Bismarck. As only three men survived that sinking it was no surprise to anyone when it was confirmed that Mr Plumpton was not one of these. His wife's only compensation to the loss of her husband was the news that the Bismarck herself had been caught and sunk by gunfire, from ships of the British Home Fleet.

Mrs Plumpton had carried on in the grocery shop until the end of the war in 1945. It was then she sold the business to Mr and Mrs Tranter. To keep herself busy she opened the Plumpton School of Dance. Her one problem with this was she could never get enough male students to attend her classes. We certainly weren't interested in this silly pursuit, and not many other boys were either.

So in Banter Wood that evening we talked over this challenge. We knew a little bit about this strange game. We had found out there were seven members of each team, and the object of the game was to score more hoops than the opposition, just like handball. So we saw no reason why we shouldn't humiliate the girls by beating them out of sight. Then we could bask in the fact they had to wait on us hand and foot for the next week.

The first thing we had to do was pick our team. This was fairly easy because we knew who the best sportsmen were in our gang. We would be captained by Davie Collins and then we would have Mickie Tranter, Johnnie White, David Callow, the tall figure of Phil Landers, Paul Edwards and me.

"We need to delegate positions," said our leader and we all agreed. So the team we finally got together was Paul Edwards as goal stopper, Mickie Tranter and Johnnie White in defence, with Davie, Phil, David and me as attackers. We were now ready to bring on the game.

None of us had any idea that the most humiliating day in the history of the Sundance Gang was going to take place the following Saturday. We took to the field, in bright sunshine and I watched the girls as they followed us out. Led by their captain Angela Ford, they were wearing the same strip, in our school colours as when they played against Brimly. We all had our PT kit of shorts and vests and couldn't wait to get started. I still couldn't see why this game had to have two referees. I suppose the fact that it's a girl's game, after all nothing girls do ever makes any sense.

We lined up facing each other and the whistle sounded to start the game. We immediately showed our male superiority. Davie dived forward, and got the ball, pushing Sheila Wilcock out of the way in doing so. He charged downfield, bouncing the ball in front of him before passing it across field to Phil Landers. He caught the ball and dodged between Irene Stapleton and Tracy Ward. From just outside their circle he lofted it high into the air. It flew straight and dropped beautifully through their hoop, one nil to us. We had been so eager to get a good start that none of us had taken any notice of the whistles that were sounding.

Miss Trout came running up to Davie and shouted at him.

"What on earth do you and your team think you're doing?" she raged at him.

"What do you mean?" asked a bemused Davie.

"You have committed at least six fouls and your goal doesn't count."

At this we all crowded round in protest. What was wrong? We had scored a very good goal and these females were trying to deny it to us.

"You," she said pointing at Davie. "Ran with the ball, bouncing it as you went, that is against the rules. You also ran out of your position. That is against the rules. You pushed an opponent out of the way. That is against the rules. You then passed across field while still running and that is also against the rules."

She then glared at Phil and told him that he cannot score. Only the designated player on each side can do that, and it can only be done from inside the circle.

"Not from way outside where you threw it."

So our goal didn't count and from the free passes that were awarded to the girls, they scored three goals that did.

The game went from bad to worse. We had been so confident of beating them none of us had bothered to read up on the rules of this game, and boy were there some rules. By half time, which was a nightmare half an hour for us, the score was sixteen to the girls and nil to us. The second half was no better, made even worse by the fact we were fed up with the continual sound of the whistle. Every time one of us moved to get the ball we were penalised for one thing or another.

I was even told off by the other referee Maisy Prendergast. I had hopped on my landing foot before throwing the ball. What was she talking about? In soccer nobody said which foot you had to land on before you could pass the ball to a team mate. Even the normally calm David Callow fell afoul of Miss Trout when she stopped him for breaking yet another rule. He kicked the ball off the court in frustration giving away two free passes to the girl's team instead of one. He was also told off for ungentlemanly behaviour.

At the end of that hour, which will go down in history for us, the score was girls thirty six, boys nil. We had to line up to receive application forms to join Miss Plumpton's dance class before we could get off that netball court. The girls smirked at us and gleefully said, "We told you so."

"Yah," said Davie. "You made up them daft rules just to get the better of us. If you'd played properly we would've beaten you easy."

It was Miss Trout who answered him. Coming up silently behind us she was quick to defend the sport.

"Those daft rules as you put it are legitimate rules of netball. We gave you and the rest of your boy's time to study them and prepare for this game. That you are so ignorant of any of them makes it obvious none of you even bothered. So you got the result you deserve. By the way we all want to see you dancing nicely at this year's Christmas party."

Needless to say our next meeting in Banter Wood was a very gloomy one. None of us could believe the humiliation we had been made to suffer by a bunch of girls. We would never live this down. Now our side of the bargain had to be kept by learning ballroom dancing. All of us who had been in the team, and the two who mercifully had not, looked at a future that was filled with nothing but gloom.

"I can see only one thing we can do about this," said Davie.

"What?" we all wanted to know.

"Think about it," he said. "Everyone thinks it's a hoot that we've got to learn to dance, and nobody thinks we'll be able to do it. So let's prove them wrong."

"What do you mean Davie?" I nervously asked.

"I mean let's learn to dance. It can't be that hard can it?"

"That's what we said about netball," Mickie Tranter reminded him.

"I know that, but she was right. We took the game for granted, we didn't bother to prepare for it, and that's why we bloody well lost. Now they all expect us to make fools of ourselves again at the Christmas party. In case you had forgotten this is to be held in Brimly village hall this year."

Every year the two villages came together to put on an open air candlelit procession. The evening ended with a wonderful party enjoyed by everyone. This year it was Brimly village that would put this on. Everyone would be there, including Frank Thornton and his gang. We couldn't do anything that would give them the slightest chance to laugh at us.

"It's now nearly the end of September," Davie went on, "which means we have three months to do it. It's not beyond us boys so let's all agree to do this thing properly."

That was why all nine of us turned up at Miss Plumpton's dancing school in our village hall the next evening. Classes went from seven thirty until nine thirty. Miss Plumpton herself was a lady none of us knew very well. Although we saw her in and around the village, she was not a person we would normally have anything to do with. We never knew her husband as we were all very small babies when he died in the war. So the first meeting with this stern looking old lady was something of an ordeal.

She had us standing in a line in front of the hall with the rest of her class, mainly girls, looking at us.

"Well everyone, as you can see we are graced this evening with nine new pupils, all of the male sex, so let's make them all feel welcome."

There was a round of applause at this. It wasn't very loud and certainly not very welcoming. The news of our humiliation at the netball match had gone all round the village. So everyone in this class knew we were here whether we liked it or not, and didn't think we genuinely wanted to learn.

Our dancing experience started with Miss Plumpton showing us the steps to the waltz. We stood in a straight line and tried to copy the ones she was showing us.

"Lead off with your right foot boys, then glide forward, bring together, step back. Now reverse, lead off with your left, glide forward, bring together and step back. Now you try, all together, with the right foot and lead off."

We all moved forward, keeping in a nice straight line.

"No, no, no," wailed Miss Plumpton. "I told you to glide forward, keeping your right foot in touch with the floor. Not take giant strides as though you were jumping over some large object."

We had automatically stepped forward which wasn't right for dancing. It took the entire first lesson to learn how to glide over the floor but eventually we achieved some sort of success. Phil Landers and Danny Meadows did better than all the rest of us put together. These two also did well in our second lesson when we were paired with girls. The rest of us had to put up with complaints about stamping on the feet of our partners. As far as I was concerned it was their own fault, they should keep their feet out of the way.

The waltz gradually took shape however, against all the odds. I could glide by now, but had no idea how to master the turns. The trouble really started when we moved on to the other dance. Miss Plumpton had decided that given the short time she had to teach us with any sort of decency, she would only deal with the waltz and the quickstep. This was, as far as I was concerned anyway, an impossible dance to perform.

We were shown the steps, "Slow slow quick quick slow," drawled our teacher as we tried to keep up with her.

With just the two exceptions of Phil and Danny we made a complete nonsense of this. Miss Plumpton was becoming more and more agitated at our continued failure to master the rudiments of this dance. She paired us off with partners and we made their lives hell as they tried to perform this quickstep with us. My feet got tangled up every time I tried to go from quick to slow.

But under the direction of the girl I was dancing with named Felicity Wentworth, I did, more to my amazement than anyone else, actually start to get this dance right. I was still not very good at spin turns, but otherwise not too bad. Davie was doing fairly well too with his partner, Julie Spooner. We were enjoying these lessons now, because dancing with girls was something that until now we hadn't experienced. To hold a girl so close, as was necessary for this, was a pleasant sensation.

We found it funny at times, none more so than the night we got far too adventurous with the quickstep. Phil and Danny were so good by now they were putting combinations of very fast steps into their routines. The rest of us watched them many times and once tried to do the same. Three couples more or less in line tried to put this new fast technique into practice.

It was a disaster of course. I was the first one to trip over my own feet, causing Felicity and I to lose our balance completely and fall in an undignified heap onto the dance floor. This was bad enough, but we were too close to Davie and his partner to our right and Johnnie White and his partner to our left. Both couples fell over as a result and six of us were now in a tangled heap on the floor. Miss Plumpton just looked at this shambles on her dance floor, then sighed and walked away. The girls, once they got over the shock, mercifully saw the funny side of things and we all ended up laughing about it.

One thing though was now certain, we had all learned enough about ballroom dancing to be able to do well at the Christmas party, especially as we would be dancing with the girls who had now become our regular partners. Losing the netball match so badly had seemed like the end of the world for us, after doing so well in the boxing ring. Now though it was starting to turn into an event we were enjoying. For Phil and Danny it was to become something they would both excel at and be very involved with in the years to come.

With Christmas taken care of now we knew our dancing skills could be shown off to the inhabitants of both villages, we gave serious thought to our next adventure on the raft. With October looming this had to be done in the next two weeks, or not at all this year. We would also be involved in collecting rubbish for the huge bonfire on November the fifth.

This was a wonderfully enjoyable time of the year for us. On that night the whole village turned out for the bonfire and fireworks display. Add to this the potatoes that were roasted in the fire and it was a perfect evening. During the lead up we had the most enormous fun with the bangers we managed to get hold of. These became hand grenades that were thrown at each other in Banter Wood. Fitting in the raft trip though would be no mean feat.

Two things happened to further delay this. The first of these was when, during the first week of October, we were told that Colonel Worthington-Pugh and Commander Phillips wanted to speak to us all. We were further surprised upon turning up for the meeting in our village hall to find Frank Thornton and his gang there as well.

"Come along in boys," the Colonel said to us, as we hesitated in the doorway.

"What are that lot doing here?" demanded Davie.

"Come along in little boy and all will be explained."

Davie hated being called little boy and scowled at the Colonel, but we all filed into the hall behind him.=

"Now then boys," he said when we were all seated. "The commander and I were most impressed with the way you performed in the boxing ring at the recent contest. We saw a lot of promise and have decided that what this area needs is a proper boxing club. A gymnasium where you can all come and train and learn new skills in the ring, and if it's a success then we will arrange matches against other clubs in the region."

There was a big response to this, both gangs thoroughly agreeing to it.

"We have spoken to all of your parents about this, and they are in agreement," said the loud voice of Commander Phillips. "But," he went on as we all cheered this piece of news. "We will need funds to set this up. Your parents have said they will help with donations, but it may not be enough. We will need proper equipment, weights, a punch ball, a full size ring etc. So you will all be given the chance to raise some much needed cash for this venture."

We looked at each other in amazement. We were only ten years old. How could we raise money? The Brimly boys looked just as confused as we did and all of us looked blankly at the Colonel and Commander Phillips.

"You all know about the raft that the Surlington boys have built," the Commander went on. "Well the Colonel and I, and incidentally most of your parents as well, believe it will be a good idea if you can get sponsorship."

"What's that?" we all wanted to know.

"Sponsorship boys," said the Commander, "is when people agree to pay you a set amount of money if you achieve whatever it is you are setting out to do. For instance, if you were going on a sponsored walk, you would be paid something like 3p a mile. So the more miles you walk the more money you earn. In your case we will work out how many nautical miles we think it is possible for you to go on that raft of yours. Your potential sponsors can then promise whatever they can afford for every mile you achieve."

We were excited about this and the noise level mounted considerably inside the hall. The Colonel finally quelled this as he shouted for order.

Davie had been looking very serious and now asked "But where do we get these sponsors?"

"From anyone you know," said the Colonel, "from your friends and neighbours, your school teachers and friends of your parents."

"I'm sure your parents will help you with getting sponsors," the Commander chipped in, "Then it will be up to you to see how far you can actually get on that raft."

"But what about us?" asked Frank Thornton, "We want to be doing something to earn money for it as well."

"Quite right," said the Commander. "And so you shall, we want you to build your own raft. Then on a set day, probably in late spring of next year, both rafts will compete against each other to see who can cover the longest distance."

"That will be us," both gangs shouted, then started insulting one another.

"Your lot won't make it to the first bend," we gleefully taunted them.

"We'll get further than that," they countered. "And it's a good job you lot can swim," they went on, "cause you always end up in the water."

"Only cause you rotten lot sabotaged us last time. All you'll see of us this time is the back of our raft as we leave you all behind."

"Alright," laughed the commander. "Remember all of you this is not a race, it is a contest to see how far you can get down the River Gest. The further you go the more money you earn. There will be no sabotage and no tricks while out on the water to try and interfere with each other's progress, is that understood?"

We nodded in agreement, but of course both gangs were already scheming to come up with some way to make sure their raft and not the enemies went furthest.

"One thing more before we end this meeting as it is now getting rather late," said Commander Phillips. "I believe you boys from this village plan to make a trip downriver on your raft fairly soon now, is that right?"

"Yes Sir," said Davie. "We're going next Saturday."

"I have to point out that this will undoubtedly turn out to be a keenly fought contest between both gangs, so with this in mind I will ask you to cancel that trip."

"Why Sir?" we all wanted to know. We were looking forward to going on the raft, and knew if we didn't do it now we would have to cancel anyway because winter was fast approaching and the water in the river would be too cold.

"Because it will give you an unfair advantage over the boys from Brimly," he explained. "They have yet to build their raft and if you set out on yours now it will give you the chance to get used to it. This must be fair in every way. When both rafts set off from the starting line, neither crew will have been out on their respective crafts before. So it will be up to you, once you are in motion on the water, to handle your raft in the way that will get the best out of her."

Reluctantly this made sense, even to us, so we agreed and the meeting broke up. As we watched the Brimly boys walking away towards the bridge that would take them back to their village, we all knew we would do whatever it took to beat them and get our raft further down the river than theirs. Our rivalry with them was so deep seated. We were aware that even now they would be scheming to not only stop us, but put us out of the contest altogether if they could.

At our next choir practice we had a visit from the Reverend Morley who told us he had made arrangements for this year's choir boys outing. We were over the moon because he decided to act on the suggestion we had made a few weeks ago, and set up a coach trip to Portsmouth's famous naval dockyard. We had been there before on Navy open day, but this would be a boat trip around the docks, looking at all the huge warships that would be tied up alongside. Some of those ships could be the ones we had heard about from the Commander when he relayed his stories of the war at sea, and what a thrill that would be.

Danny Meadows was particularly excited about this because he really did want to go into the Navy when he grew up. He would have problems here though because his dad wanted Danny to follow him into the banking business. It was an awkward situation. Danny's grandad had been a high ranking naval officer, and the sea was already pulsating through his veins. Commander Phillips had promised Danny he would see what he could do if Mr. Meadows denied him the chance to follow his dream of going to sea in Britain's Royal Navy.

The morning of the outing dawned bright and clear and we were in a high state of excitement upon boarding the coach. There were sandwiches that our mother's had provided and we would have dinner and tea in Portsmouth. This was paid for by the church and what could be better than that? There were eighteen of us altogether in the choir, which meant the entire Sundance Gang was there, as well as nine of our school and village mates. The Reverend Morley was in charge, assisted by Miss Trump.

The trip down to Portsmouth wasn't a long one, as it wasn't that far away. But with eighteen boys on board, the coach was certainly noisy. When we arrived Danny was beside himself with excitement as he looked at the magnificent and majestic warships in their berths at this illustrious dockyard.

"Look," he kept shouting as he pointed at one ship after another.

"Alright Danny," laughed Davie. "We can all see them."

Danny had been so excited on the way down he hadn't even eaten the sandwiches his mother had made for him but we helped him out there.

The Reverend and Miss Trump, both now looking a bit haggard, organized us into groups of two and we marched off to the jetty. Waiting for us there was a man who could only be described as an old sea dog. He was in charge of the motor launch that would take us on a magical trip of adventure around the ships. A wonderful view from seaward of the pride of Britain's navy.

He was an old man with a scraggy grey beard, and a clay pipe in his mouth which jutted out at right angles to his jaw. Davie and I turned away because we couldn't stop laughing. He looked just like the cartoon character Popeye. We were still laughing as we got aboard the launch, but once underway this old man of the sea showed us that no matter what he looked like, he certainly knew his business. Every ship we came up to, he named and gave a short history of.

We saw giant aircraft carriers, big cruisers and the fascinating destroyers that were so fast over the water and did so much to help in our victory over Germany. It wasn't only Danny who was jumping up and down with excitement as we identified the ships that Commander Phillips had told us about.

We all shouted out as we saw the Battleship HMS Vanguard. This was the one he had served on and been in action with during the recent conflict. Now we were looking at her and passing right under her superstructure. We saw other ships that day that had survived World War Two. There was the Destroyer Battleaxe, the Cruiser Devonshire, plus two aircraft carriers, Illustrious and Roberts. To see them and be able to marvel at their sheer size, especially the carriers was awesome. There really was no way to describe how we all felt, seeing these ships that had fought in the war, and others that had been built in the six years since. It was a day none of us were ever likely to forget.

We heard later that Danny had been so full of this he had hardly stopped talking about it for the next week. His father finally ran out of patience and told Danny in no uncertain terms, that he could forget any plans he might be harbouring about joining the Navy.

"You can forget all that nonsense," he had told his son. "You will be coming into the banking business with me. You have the potential to make it as big as I have done, and becoming a manager in time. Work boy. That is the key," he stormed.

Poor Danny was so down in the dumps over this and we tried to cheer him up. But not even our efforts would help. He hated the idea of working in a bank so much. The bank staff always treated him with respect and saw he wasn't kept waiting when he needed to speak to his father. But there was always this feeling of being stifled. He could never see himself working the long hours his dad did in this gloomy atmosphere.

Unknown to us he went back to speak to Commander Phillips about it, and got the promise he wanted to hear. "I don't know if I can do any good Danny," he was told. "But I will go and see your father and put your side of this to him."

That meeting took place three days later. Commander Phillips came into the manager's office at the bank and was greeted in the way all clients were, with a polite, "Good morning Commander, please sit down."

Mr Meadows then took his place behind the desk.

"Now Commander I have your account details before me, how can I help you today?"

"This is somewhat delicate. You see I am not here about my account, but to talk to you about your young son Danny."

"My son?" asked a surprised Mr Meadows "what about him?"

"He has come to ask me if I can intervene in your decision to have him follow you into the same business."

The bank manager sprang to his feet in anger and burst out. "Really Commander, you are interfering in family matters that have nothing at all to do with you. Furthermore you come to the bank to talk to me about them. I can only discuss banking business here, and I will not talk about personal affairs with anyone at anytime. Good morning sir," he finished, glaring at the door of his little office.

The Commander didn't react to this however but said quietly, "I understand your anger sir, but I promised young Danny I would do all I could to help him and the least you can do is hear me out."

"I am not interested in anything you have to say," raged the now furious bank manager. "Kindly leave my office at once."

"I came to speak to you and speak to you I will," said the naval officer in the voice he used when giving orders aboard her majesty's ships of war. "Sit down sir," he ordered.

The tone of his voice got through to Mr Meadows and he slowly sat down again behind his desk.

"I have done a lot of research since young Danny first came to me with this, and I was somewhat surprised to find he is the grandson of the much respected Admiral C. J. Meadows. He is a man I have had the pleasure of serving with and I know how much he is liked and respected throughout the British fleet. I don't know why you didn't follow him into the service, but that of course is your own business. But young Danny, at the tender age of ten years is showing that he has salt water running through his veins. He longs to go to sea, not in the Merchant service, but in the Royal Navy.

He talked to me about his grandad in a way that showed how much he admires him and wants to emulate him. You are his father, and his future is of course in your hands. He is an obedient boy and will do as you ask, but I beg you to see things through his eyes. He will come into the bank, but he will hate it. He will gaze at the sea and, I'm sure, join up as soon as he comes of age.

I would like your permission to enrol him now in the junior section of Westbridge Sea Cadets. From there he will find out himself if this is what he really wants, and if it is I further ask your permission to do all I can to get him into Dartmouth Royal Navy College. I believe sir that he already has the leadership qualities that his famous grandfather has. He may not be the leader of the boys' gang he now belongs to, but I recognise in him the ability to make decisions and this is so vital when commanding men."

This long statement was followed by a considerable silence during which Mr Meadows stood up and went to the window of his office, turning his back on Commander Phillips.

With his back still turned he finally spoke, "That's quite a speech Commander and you have given me a lot to think about. You're right about Admiral Meadows. He is my father and I am very proud of him, however I never wanted to be near the sea.

I will ask you to understand please that any decision I make about my son I do for his own good. Every father wants his son to follow him, especially if he himself has been successful. I have listened to you and while doing so remembered for the first time in many years, my father trying to influence me to go into the navy. I held out against him and fortunately managed to make my own way in the banking business. I seem to be doing the same thing to my own son as my father did to me. I will contact you in the next few days with my decision about this. But for now Commander I really do wish you good morning."

Two days after this meeting in the bank Danny burst into the hideout.

"I'm going to join the sea cadets," he said, a grin spreading right across his face.

"What?" we all shouted. "What are you talking about?"

"My dad told me just now," he said. "I was just leaving when he called me back. He said Commander Phillips had spoken to him about me, and though he wasn't very happy about it he said I could join the sea cadets and we'll see where we go from there. Isn't it terrific?"

"How are you going to join the sea cadets?" we all wanted to know.

"The commander said he'll see to it, there's a branch in Westbridge, and he said if any of you lot want to join he'll get you in as well."

We needed no persuasion to know this was an adventure none of us wanted to miss, so went to see the commander at the first opportunity. From there began a quest that would change one of our gang members lives forever.

Chapter 9

Approaching Westbridge there was a feeling of excitement running through us all. We were a little scared too because we didn't know what was in front of us. Commander Phillips had arranged for us to receive application forms, which our parents helped us fill out. The sea cadets were run by adult volunteers. They gave boys such as us the chance to enjoy land and water pursuits that we wouldn't normally have the opportunity to do.

We were greeted by Mr Leadbetter the cadet leader. He shook hands with my dad who had driven us here in his van. We were then welcomed and introduced to the other members of the troop. Reading out our names he stopped when he came to Danny's.

"Danny Meadows? No relation to the great Admiral Meadows I suppose?"

"He's my grandad sir,"

"Is he indeed? Then we will be expecting great things from you."

Commander Phillips had taken the trouble to warn Danny he could expect this reaction wherever he went.

"When you're related to someone who is as famous and successful as your grandad you will find it's an advantage and a disadvantage all rolled into one. The name of Meadows will open doors for you as you progress in the Navy. But if you don't shape up to people's expectations, all of that will work against you. Admiral Meadows was as famous in his day as the great Lord Nelson. He had the ability of leadership that so many people lack. There are few people who can do this. To have men that loved and trusted him enough to follow him in battles that seem impossible to overcome yet win through because of the faith they have in him. After the war he was, rightly so, decorated by his Majesty King George 6th"."

Danny had much to live up to but was game for the challenge, and he knew we would always be there to help him in any situation.

On that first day we were all issued with uniforms, only David Callow had worn one before. In his case it was a scout's outfit whenever he turned up for their weekly meetings. It meant a good deal to us as we got changed and paraded outside, now all dressed the same way in navy blue, with matching hats that had Westbridge Sea cadets on the brim.

None of us will ever forget the sight of Danny Meadows. That day he became a completely different person as soon as he stood in sea cadet uniform. He had been born for this, his grandad's blood ran through his veins and his destiny was there for all to see. The second Admiral Meadows had one foot on the ladder of promotion. It might take him many years to achieve this, but we knew he would get there and meet his dream in the service of the Royal Navy.

We spent two nights a week as well as most weekends attending the sea cadets. None of the rest of us had any desire to go into the Navy proper, but enjoyed the challenges that this threw at us. The small boat training was especially good because it would really help us in our raft race against the Brimly boys next year. We also learned the art of tying knots. Previously we had relied on the expertise of David Callow for this, but now we would be able to do it ourselves.

Many new friendships began as the rest of the Westbridge troop learned about the raft race and wanted to know what our chances were. They tried to give Danny a hard time. Saluting him whenever they had to pass by they would say "Good morning, afternoon or evening Admiral," whichever suited the time of day.

Danny had seen his grandad many times in his young life so when this happened he simply returned the salute and then went on with whatever he was doing at the time. This eventually got through to everyone and the teasing stopped. Danny had learned the first lesson on the way to a career in the Navy. Stand up for yourself and don't be put down by anyone. We were already proud of him for this.

We also had duties to perform for our village and coming up was one of the two biggest occasions of the year. Both villages combined to celebrate these, namely bonfire night and Christmas. Whichever village hosted November 5th, it was then the duty of the other one to put on the big Christmas procession and party. So with all the rest of the children of Surlington, we spent some evenings collecting rubbish for the huge bonfire that was put up in the middle of our village square. Branches of dead wood that were lying about in Banter Wood, along with cardboard boxes from our various parents and neighbours were collected.

On the night Surlington village was lit up by the flames of the bonfire and a big firework display. It was one of the few times in the year when the Brimly gang enjoyed themselves along with us. All rivalry was put aside during these two occasions and we joined in the fun together. Baking potatoes in the fire and then laughing as we ate these blackened vegetables.

It was also an important night for me as I was enjoying my tenth birthday. Being born on so famous a date had brought a lot of laughter when I entered the world. All my relatives told my parents they would never be stuck about what to buy me for my birthday.

"Just get him a load of fireworks," they all laughed. I always did get these, and enjoyed them every year with my friends, while my parents made sure I got proper birthday presents as well.

This year there was to be a big party, held in the public bar of the Dog and Duck. Children were not usually allowed in here, not even me and I lived at the pub. Tonight though was special and all of us were there, along with the Brimly gang. Dad had decided to turn this into a fancy dress party, and after the fireworks display he was once more behind the bar of his pub. But not wearing his usual clothes.

My mum had helped both dad and me to dress up as the American superheroes Batman and Robin. She had copied the costumes from the comics I had. Dad was dressed in a light blue pair of pyjamas, and had a pair of dark blue bathers which he wore over the top of these. She also made him a dark blue cape, just like the real Batman. I had the same sort of costume, in my case a pair of green pyjamas and red bathers worn outside of these and a red cape. This was approved by everyone and got a lot of laughter.

The evening was going really well when the door of the bar suddenly opened and a gang of bikers, who had been causing a lot of trouble in the district during the past few weeks burst in. Their leader was a big rough looking man, with a short beard. He swaggered into the bar and six more dirty looking men, all in leather jackets and filthy jeans followed him. They came up to the counter and pushed their way to the front, several of our regular customers along with many of our guests being rudely shoved out of their way.

Dad wanted to go round and throw them out, but mum urged caution.

"You can't handle these by yourself," she told him. The big man ordered drinks all round for his gang. Dad served him with seven pints of bitter then charged him way over the price for them. He reacted with expected venom and demanded to know why the drinks cost so much.

"They don't normally," dad calmly told him, "only to vermin like you."

That there was going to be trouble was now obvious and all of the adults with children moved into the private bar out of harm's way. All of the Brimly gang as well as the rest of our lot were among these. I was on the other side of the room, collecting glasses when these thugs came in and as I reached the bar to hand these to my mother she said, "Come round here Billy, quickly."

The urgency in her voice propelled me into action and I shot round behind the bar.

The bikers had taken their drinks and moved to one of the tables. Ada Bumstead and her gels were sitting at the next table and they turned on her, angry about the fact they had been overcharged for their drinks, though they shouldn't have been. They were the sort of people nobody wanted in their pubs, so overcharging was a sure fire way of getting rid of them. Their nasty leader looked at Miss Bumstead and snarled.

"What are you looking at you dried up old prune?" She may be a no nonsense lady but even she had never been spoken to like this before. She was visibly shaken, as were her gels, but the bikers were all laughing.

Before anyone knew what was happening the imposing figure of Colonel Worthington-Pugh appeared.

"How dare you speak to a lady in that fashion you filthy lout."

Immediately three of the thugs jumped up and shouted, "What's it got to do with you Grandad?" before punching this gallant old soldier. He would have been badly hurt because he was certainly a lot older than his attackers, and there were three of them and only one of him.

That is until the booming voice of Mr Collins, our village blacksmith and Davies dad, rang out. "Step away from him."

The thugs attacking the Colonel paused to consider this. What they saw was a much younger and bigger man facing them. They stopped and made to sit down, but the other four of their mates stood up and all seven now faced Mr Collins. I could see Davie looking anxiously from his vantage point in the private bar.

"Oh so you think seven of you are enough to beat me, do you? Well come on then."

The action that followed was so swift it took him by surprise. All of these horrible bikers rushed forward and he went down to the floor under a mass of bodies. There was such a struggle going on it was impossible to see what was happening. But everyone knew that our likeable village blacksmith was somewhere underneath and likely to be hurt if help didn't arrive quickly.

It did. My dad had been watching things very closely indeed and now saw his friend and neighbour in big trouble. With no hesitation at all, before my mum could protest, he jumped up onto the bar and launched himself at the heaving mass of bodies on the floor. He was still wearing his Batman outfit and the cape bloomed out behind him as he flew through the air, making him look just like the real caped crusader. It was said many times afterwards it was this sight that so unnerved the bikers. Dad let out a yell as he jumped and looking up they could see this caped apparition flying towards them.

The result of this was three of them breaking off straight away and trying to run out of the door. Their progress was interrupted by Miss Bumstead and the Colonel who tripped them up. That's when I came into my own. I too jumped on the bar counter and let fly at them with a jet of soda water from the siphon I had grabbed.

My soda stream hit the first two on the back of their heads while the third one made the mistake of looking round to see where this new threat was coming from. What he saw was a boy dressed as Robin squirting soda water at him. His mouth dropped open in surprise and my aim was straight and true. I squirted the water right into his gaping mouth and he nearly choked on it. All three of these now ran out of the bar and the Colonel shouted to me, "Well done lad, I'm proud of you."

The other four now had no chance at all, my dad and Mr Collins made short work of them and I will never forget the beautiful punch that Davies dad landed on the obnoxious leader of this gang of louts. He reeled backwards and landed flat on his back. He was then pulled to his feet and, along with the other three, quite literally thrown out of the bar into the street.

Now everyone converged on these horrible intruders to our village and they lost no time at all in jumping on their motor bikes and roaring off in the opposite direction from which they came. Their departure was heralded by loud cheers and these particular thugs never came back this way again.

Back in the bar of the Dog and Duck my dad was apologising to everyone and telling them the party would now continue. My mum told him off for the way he had flown into the fight.

"You could have been badly hurt," she said. "And you," looking at me, "What were you thinking of?"

"Don't shout at him Martha," dad said. "He was alright from where he was standing and his soda water helped a lot. Mike Collins could have been hurt and he's been both a friend and neighbour of ours for a lot of years. I couldn't just leave him in a situation like that."

"Men," my mother said, then looking at both of us "like father like son." She stalked off into the private bar and dad winked at me.

"Don't take any notice of that Billy, she was worried that's all, underneath she's proud of both of us."

Davie was standing close to his dad. He had been scared when he saw him disappear under the weight of so many bodies, before the combined efforts of the Taylor boys came to the rescue.

The evening just got better from there. Everyone quickly got over the trouble and laughed at the way it had turned out. Miss Bumstead, the Colonel and of course Mr Collins had been treated to a free drink for their help in the affray, and I had a large lemonade and a pork pie as my reward.

It was Frank Thornton, of all people, who said it was a good job Batman and Robin had been around. At first this was received with silence until everyone saw what he meant. They pictured my dad flying from the bar, his cape flowing out behind him as he dived to help Mr Collins. Then me in my costume, doing my bit from the bar top. The chorus of Batman and Robin to the rescue rang out and the laughter went on and on. My mum even joined in. The danger had passed and she was over her fright that her husband and son might be hurt so could very definitely see the funny side of this whole affair.

The day after bonfire night one thing was on my mind. Now ten years old I could reasonably expect my parents to let me have the one thing every boy of my age wanted, my first pair of long trousers.

Three other members of the Sundance gang had their birthdays before the end of the year, Davie Collins, Mickie Tranter, and Phil Landers. The others would pass this landmark age in the first month of the New Year. One of us was sure to achieve this very important cycle in his life first. Phil Landers was growing so fast his legs seemed to be longer every time we saw them. This made him look even more ridiculous and he was desperate to get his long trousers as soon as he could.

As Christmas approached most of our evenings were divided between the sea cadets and Miss Plumpton's dancing school. We were getting more relaxed now as we put together, under her expert guidance, a surprise performance for the big Christmas party. There was some good natured taunting about our dancing from the girls. This was fair enough, we had not bothered to find out about a game they were very good at. Because of this we lost badly. In a way though maybe this was a good thing, none of us would have ever gone anywhere near ballroom dancing otherwise. As we got better we began to enjoy it and were now really looking forward to our first public performance.

At sea cadets we did a lot of small boat handling and were absolutely at home on the water by now. This was ideal preparation for the big raft challenge next year. My parents had let all of our regulars know about this and the fact we needed sponsorship for getting as far down the course as we could. The proceeds would go towards the new boxing club, proposed by Colonel Worthington-Pugh and Lieutenant Commander Phillips.

The response had been wonderful. Just two weeks after asking for financial help, dad worked out that if we got to the end of the marked course, now three miles further than our original journey, we would get the enormous sum of 2/6d from each one of our sponsors who had pledged to give us 6d a mile.

"Now," said dad after breakfast one morning. "If you go all the way to the finish line, at the moment with 34 sponsors pledging 6d a mile you will make £4.5/s."

This was such a huge amount of money and when I told the rest of the gang they were over the moon about it. Especially since some of their own friends and relatives had also agreed to sponsor us, so we now stood to make over £5.00.

"I can't see Frank Thornton's lot beating that," said Davie. "So we must make sure that not only do we go further than them, but that we do it front of them."

At our next sea cadet meeting another surprise awaited us. We were asked about the raft challenge. Mr Leadbetter told us the course was set to go past the three masted training ship, which we had seen many times from our side of the River Gest.

"You will all be going aboard her soon," he told us, and the excitement we felt at this news was tremendous. "From her deck you'll be able to see the finishing line which is already marked out further up the river. Now what is the other raft you'll be going up against like?"

This time it wasn't Davie who answered but Danny Meadows. "We don't know sir. We're not allowed to go over their side of the river to look at it. We've been told this would be cheating. Both rafts have to be untried before either crew sets out on this challenge."

The fact it was Danny who spoke up was not lost on Mr Leadbetter.

"Ah the Admirals grandson again is it?"

"Yes Sir," grinned Danny.

"Alright then, we will naturally support you so I want permission for myself and a few of the lads to come and have a look at your raft. After which we will talk about the amount of sponsorship we as a group will give."

We greeted this news with a huge cheer, Danny it was who gave permission for the inspection of our raft. There seemed no limit now on the amount of money we could earn towards the boxing club.

"I have spoken to Commander Philips about the club this money is going towards, and it's a very good cause," Mr Leadbetter told us. "The boys from the sea cadets will also be involved and we can organise inter cadet contests around the country. It's a great idea and we all want to be a part of it. Incidentally Commander Phillips and Captain Henderson RN, the Commander of HMS Dragon ,the training ship you will all be aboard next week, are old comrades. They served together during the last war."

This news was even better. We would be serving under, even if only in a junior capacity, a man who had fought in World War Two.

Mr Leadbetter, along with eight senior members of our sea cadet force met us in Banter Wood three days later. Our raft had been moored for the past month and a half ready to go in the great raft challenge. They went over every inch of it, from the logs to the barrels and carriage. To our enormous delight they could find nothing wrong with it having only nice things to say about its construction. Some of them even said that in future they should be taking lessons from us.

"The raft is great boys," Mr Leadbetter said. "With your sail up, you should go a long way. But this river can be treacherous and does have strong currents. We want you to complete the course. This isn't a race is it?"

This time Davie answered and said, "Not strictly speaking sir, but we have a long standing dispute with the boys from Brimly village and they will want to not only go further than us but do it in a better time. That's what we want as well, so as far as we're concerned this is very much a race."

"I see," said Mr Leadbetter, a grin spreading across his face. "Are you allowed to use paddles?"

We all nodded.

"Very well then, we will teach you how to do that for maximum effect. I'll organize classes out on the river in our boats where you can get used to using nothing but paddles. But," he went on, "and it's a very big but. Everything we teach you we will also teach your rivals, otherwise you will have an unfair advantage over them. Do you all agree?"

A chorus of "Yes sir" greeted this.

"Very well then, leave the rest to me and be prepared for some vigorous training in the next few weeks."

We went home very happy that night. The Navy was going to help us with the raft and with Christmas fast approaching we had a point to prove here as well. First though we wanted to know how much of a challenge the Brimly lot would put up against us.

"It would be good if we could see how they get on with the paddle classes," Davie mused.

"Why can't we?" asked Danny Meadows.

"Because we're not allowed to watch are we?"

"No, but our girls can," Danny reminded him. "Do you remember Angela Ford told us the Brimly girls are always watching us. Well that means they'll see when we're out on the water and report back. Angela originally said she and the rest of our girls would keep watch for us the next time we went out on our raft, to make sure that lot over there don't get a chance to mess things up again. Well they won't have to do that now will they cause Frank Thornton and his gang will be out there on their raft alongside us. So why don't we ask the girls to spy on the Brimlys paddling exploits for us?"

This was quite a long speech for the normally quiet Danny and after just a few seconds Davie said, "Well done Danny, I'll speak to Angela tomorrow."

The next day everything was set up nicely, the girls having agreed readily enough to spy on the Brimlys for us.

Our thoughts turned back to Christmas and what we would be performing for both villages in Brimly's hall. Our girls, along with Miss Trout, would be hoping for another laugh at our expense. We may have made the mistake of thinking girls were no good at ball games, now they in their turn thought boys were hopeless at dancing.

Coming into December tempers were starting to fray as we tried to put the finishing touches to our routine. Finally Miss Plumpton got us all together.

"Now listen all of you, there is no need for this frustration. All of you have worked miracles in the past few weeks and you are so close to putting on a very good show together. Your only enemy now is yourselves. Only you think you can't do it, and that's why we're seeing so many unnecessary mistakes. Slow down, think about what you're doing, get the timing right, and on the night I will be so very proud of you all."

My regular dancing partner Felicity Wentworth also gave me a lot of encouragement.

"Keep going as you are Billy," she whispered to me. "You're getting better all the time."

Coming from Felicity this was praise indeed and I felt a lovely warm glow pass right through me. She and I were fast becoming more than just dancing partners. We were now firm friends as well. I never thought I could feel such friendship for a girl, but it was happening and I liked the feeling it gave me.

During the week before Christmas it snowed almost continually and our whole district was covered with a thick layer of white. We looked forward to the holidays when we would be out on our sledges and having a great time. Before that of course we had the celebrations, and the whole of our village, as well as Brimly was decorated with streamers that went from window to window across the street. Turvy Mill looked like a magical fairy grotto and was lit up with lanterns that shone and reflected in the white paint we had all helped to apply. Our pub the Dog and Duck had decorations up in both bars and looked wonderful.

On the evening of the 24th everyone from our village, both grown-ups and children, walked to the very edge of Surlington. There we were met by the inhabitants of Brimly. Lighting candles we formed up in pairs and started the procession that would take us across the bridge, over the Gest and down to the Church of the Ascension in Brimly High Street.

Carols were sung and the tones of 'Silent Night', 'Oh come all ye faithful' and other popular songs rang across the cold night air. Every year this Christmas procession excited me so much. We filed into church for the evening service and were not surprised to see Frank Thornton and co in the choir. A fair hearing was given but our overall opinion was they were nowhere near as good at it as we were.

The next day, after the wonderful surprises that were found in our Christmas presents, we made our way once more across to our neighbours village for the annual party. Upon arriving at the village hall however, all nine of us disappeared into the room behind the stage. There we found the girls waiting for us and they looked so good in their dancing dresses, all of them wearing sparkling white gowns that had pink sequins stitched all over them. Since there was only one room in which we could change, the girls were told to turn their backs as we got out of our own clothes. Then we put on long black trousers, crisp white shirts with black bow ties, over which were worn black jackets with two tails at the back. With black lightweight shoes as well we looked grand, and were now as ready as we were likely to be for the ordeal that faced us.

When Felicity turned round and saw me she said straight away, “Oh Billy you look wonderful.”

I blushed at this but managed to tell her that she too was looking superb.

Miss Plumpton now stood looking us all over.

“Well I’ve done all I can and taught you enough to go out there and give a credible performance. You look marvellous, now go out there and do me and yourselves proud.”

With this she gave us the thumbs up sign then went out of the room. We were ready to follow her, but had to wait for our introduction first. My stomach was a knot as I stood waiting. I, more than any of the others, had made mistakes during training for this performance. If it went wrong out there it would be my fault and my mistakes would be seen by everyone present, including my own parents. I was getting in such a state about this and was surprised when Felicity took my hand.

I gave her a startled look, but she smiled at me and said quietly, "You'll be fine." Incredibly as soon as she said that I relaxed and listened to Miss Plumpton out in the hall.

"A few months ago a group of boys lost a netball match and because of that had to come to me to learn how to dance. They were raw and knew nothing about the art of dancing. Today I am proud to stand here before you and introduce The Surlington Junior Formation Dance Team."

Davie and his partner then led us out onto the dance floor and there were gasps all round at our appearance. The girls lined up to the right while we lined up facing them.

The music started and the girls curtseyed while we bowed. We then moved together and started the waltz, keeping to the right steps and remembering the twists and turns as we glided in and out and around each other. Nobody made any mistakes at all and I was over the moon. Even when the music changed and became faster for the quick-step sequence, I was ready for it. Seven couples in a ring, doing regular steps, while in the centre Phil Landers and Danny Meadows, with their partners, were doing all the clever stuff. After this we went back to the waltz before finishing with a flourish as we all went into a series of spins.

As we stood, breathless now, there was a curious silence. Then it was shattered as applause rang out from all around the hall. Our parents along with everyone else's were on their feet clapping us and cheering loudly. I looked at Felicity and she positively glowed at me.

"I told you you'd be alright," she said.

I was so proud I couldn't speak, so I just smiled back at her.

Davie and the rest were just as pleased and it showed. We were suddenly surrounded and being clapped on the back by so many people. Miss Trout and the girl's netball team congratulated us all, and while doing so Angela whispered that they would be keeping an eye out for the Brimly boys whenever they were out on the water. Miss Plumpton hugged each and every one of us, boys as well as girls and just kept saying "Well done. Well done."

Even Frank Thornton's lot were nodding to us and smiling, blimey wonders will never cease.

Back at the Dog and Duck that night it went very late into the evening, well past my usual bedtime. I, along with the rest of the formation team, and all of our parents, were having a celebration of our own, so proud were they all of the way we had performed. It was gone midnight and I was yawning, trying to keep my eyes open when I felt my dad's arm around me.

We were standing in the doorway of the public bar watching everyone making their way home when he said, "Billy boy, I'm very proud of you. You showed tonight that you and the rest of your gang are up to taking on a challenge. You did so well with your dancing. Now show us all what you're made of and win that raft race."

It had started snowing again and as I watched the flakes falling to earth I replied. "You can count on us dad," and I meant it.

Chapter 10

It was nearly the end of January before our paddle training could begin. The snow had lingered and with ice forming on the water we could do nothing but wait. This didn't really put us out too much. We had so much fun out on our sledges and skating on the frozen pond in the village. We had plenty of time to do this because school was closed due to frozen pipes giving us an unscheduled holiday.

We may not have been able to go out in the boats but we did get on board HMS Dragon for the first time. Mr Leadbetter formed us all up and inspected our uniforms. None of us had any trouble passing this inspection because our mother's always made sure we were clean and tidy at all times. At least when we started out that was. Today it was important that we were immaculate because we were in sea cadet uniform and going to be presented to a Royal Navy Captain.

We were picked up and taken by coach to the side of the grand old ship. We had seen her many times before of course, living nearby as we all did. But none of us ever thought we would get this close. She was an exact replica of an eighteenth century Navy frigate and was painted in black and gold. The deck we were standing on looked spotless and towering above us were the three masts. Poor Phil looked sick as he gazed at the sheer height of them.

"Don't worry Phil," whispered Danny. "We aren't allowed to go aloft until we're fourteen at least."

This news was received with a great deal of relief, before Mr Leadbetter yelled at us.

"Captain on deck. Attention."

We snapped to as we had been taught and the figure of Captain Henderson, commander of HMS Dragon strode up to where we were all standing. He was such an impressive sight in his navy blue uniform, with four gold stripes on each arm and gold leaf around the brim of his naval cap.

"Good morning young gentlemen," he greeted us. "Welcome aboard HMS Dragon. We are always pleased to have cadets aboard, and I hope your visit today will be as enjoyable to you as it will undoubtedly be to us. Please ask any questions about anything you don't understand."

We had been well drilled about what would happen next. "The Captain," Mr Leadbetter had told us, "will then want to meet you all personally. He will come up to you one at a time, and have a short talk with you. When he appears in front of you the drill is always the same. You will salute then offer your right hand for the Captain to shake. Listen to what he has to say to you and answer any questions he may ask."

As we waited for our turn to speak to Captain Henderson, many thoughts passed through our minds and tension began to creep in. What will he say to me? The Captain strode up and down the line inspecting our uniforms. Finally he said, "Well done Mr Leadbetter, a very smart troop. They do you proud."

He then started his personal appraisal of each and every one of us. I watched and listened as he talked, first to Davie, then Johnnie White, and suddenly he was standing in front of me.

My right hand shot up to a point just above my right eye, then down smartly again to my side. Extending my right arm I shook hands with this distinguished naval officer.

"And what's your name?"

"Billy Taylor sir."

"Ah, the publican's son."

I couldn't help it, my mouth just gaped open. How did he know my dad ran the pub? The Captain just laughed.

"Commander Phillips and I are old friends, he has told me about every one of you. I have been in the Dog and Duck, and very nice it is too."

"Thank you very much sir," I stammered.

"That's alright," he replied and then amazed me even more, "Robin I believe?"

Everyone laughed out loud at this and my cheeks flamed as red as my cape had been that night in November. This important man knew all about the fight with the bikers and the part I had played in it.

When the Captain reached Danny he stopped and looked at him for a few minutes before offering his hand.

"Young Danny Meadows. I had the privilege of serving with your grandfather during the last war. He is a great man and a great leader. If you turn out to be anything like him then you have a wonderful future in the navy."

"Thank you sir," said a proud Danny. "I'll do my best."

"I'm sure you will."

After meeting and speaking to the rest of our gang and the other members of the troop, he turned to our leader.

"Carry on please Mr Leadbetter," he said before striding off and going below.

We were now treated to a marvellous tour of this grand frigate. The sails were described in detail, from the top sails that were known as topsels, to the fore, main and mizzen masts. We were shown the raised quarter deck and the huge wheel that steered the ship. Going below we saw the gun deck, the ports from where cannons fired broadsides at enemy vessels. Here we were told about the role of boys our age when a ship went into action.

The Petty Officer conducting the tour asked us if we had ever been called naughty little monkeys before. When we replied yes to this, he asked if we knew why the word monkey was used when referring to small boys. None of us knew the answer to this.

"When a ship like this went into action every cannon was manned by a crew. Their job was to load the gun ready for firing, which would be done by the gun captain. But before the cannon could be fired he had to have a special charge of powder that was brought up from the magazine by boys, most of whom were only your age. They were known throughout the British fleet as powder monkeys. Many of these boys died in battle trying to reach their appointed gun. So the name of monkey has stuck with young boys ever since."

This was fascinating and from there we saw the crews sleeping decks, where they hung their hammocks at night and ate their meals during the day. Finally was the galley where the food was cooked, and here we had the time of our lives, eating the big helpings of sausages chips and beans that were placed in front of us.

Before leaving that day the Captain reappeared and told us the whole ship would be sponsoring us in the raft race, and if we went the whole course we would be paid at least £5.00 as a result.

"And mind you win," he grinned at us.

On the way back we worked out that if we did get all the way to the finish line, we would be getting more than £12.00 in sponsorship money to give as our contribution to the

Surlington boxing club. All of us now were determined we would achieve this, no matter what it took.

The next day saw us out on the water for our first lesson in the art of paddling. This had sounded easy when Mr Leadbetter first told us about it. We would be using one of the big boats that we had already been on when rowing. My problem was the sheer size of the oar, it was bigger than me and I couldn't handle it properly. Fortunately Mickie Tranter was roughly the same size and was having the same trouble. The obvious solution was to put us both together on the same oar.

Today though, we had large paddles that looked like big table tennis bats. Instead of a rounded edge these had a sharp point. It looked easy but we were in for a shock. This was a big boat, and it was very heavy. Trying to get it to move forward using these paddles was next to impossible. Our cause was not helped by the fact we were all over the place and not digging our paddles into the water together. We had no rhythm at all and our boat was going nowhere. As for me I pushed my paddle too deep and the pull of the water nearly wrenched it out of my hand, I hung on and almost went overboard as a result.

I was saved from this embarrassment by Davie who grabbed onto me and pulled me back. Mr. Leadbetter was not pleased at this miserable failure, but assured us that it was really easy and we would get the hang of it. However, when on our third attempt there was no sign of improvement, even our troop leader was becoming impatient.

We sat gloomily in Phil Landers bedroom, in the cottage next to Turvy Mill. It was still much too cold to use our hideout in Banter wood. Davie had been asking what we could do to improve this situation.

"If we do it like that on the raft, we'll not only come in a miserable second, it's doubtful we'll get anywhere near the finish.

We knew this was right, the only consolation we had were reports coming from Angela and the girls that the Brimly lot were no better than us, and were having the same sort of trouble. They had started their training behind us as a representative from the sea cadets had to go to their village and speak to their parents, about taking their sons out on the water for the same sort of instruction in the art of paddling as we were getting. The Brimly villagers were suspicious of the offer at first and hesitated, before finally being convinced that their boys would have a better chance if they learned this art. So they were on their second try when our girls told us they were going nowhere, except round in circles.

Danny Meadows suddenly spoke up in a quiet voice and answered Davies statement. "We're not together, that's what's wrong."

"What do you mean, we're not together?" demanded Davie.

"Have you ever seen films of natives when they're out paddling their long canoes?" asked Danny. "They all dip their paddles in the water at exactly the same time, and they do it time and time again. That's what Mr Leadbetter is always shouting at us, get together, and every time we don't do it right."

"Ok," said Davie. "What can we do about it?"

"Practice."

"We do," I said, "every time we go out in the boat."

"I don't mean in the boat," Danny replied, "I mean here and now."

We looked at him, wondering what he meant when he quite literally took over the meeting.

"Come on everyone," he shouted. "Grab hold of anything you can find that will act as a paddle."

A few minutes later we all had something. Davie was using Phil's tennis racket, while the rest of us had various toys that had been lying about on the floor.

"Now," said Danny, "Let's do it all together. Watch the person in front of you and dip your paddle into the water at the same time he does, let's give it a try."

For the rest of the afternoon those toys went in and out of the water so many times we lost count. But Danny kept us at it and it was easy to see he was destined to follow his grandad into the navy. The next time we did it for real mistakes were still made, but there was a smile on Mr Leadbetter's face because he could see the improvement in us.

"Keep this up lads," he said as we disembarked from the boat, "and you'll be fine on the raft."

The only thing not making us laugh now was news that Brimly were also improving so we were going to have a race on our hands in two months time. The raft challenge was set for the middle of April, as the weather was bound to be warmer by then. We didn't mind one way or the other. Being used to the cold and certainly no strangers to getting wet, April was fine with all of us.

During February we were in class being taken by Miss Trout when Miss Tuttle came in. She was holding a handkerchief to her face and her eyes were red.

"She's been crying," Davie whispered to me, and I could see he was right.

"I'm sorry Miss Trout," she said. "But I have some rather bad news to give to the class. Children, it is my unpleasant duty to tell you that our beloved King George 6th died peacefully in his sleep last night."

We sat in stunned silence at this news, unable to take it in. The King was dead, surely not. Danny Meadows was visibly shaken, and was still in a state of shock in the playground later. Although the news about the King had shocked us we were resilient children who soon got over things like that, so Davie asked him why he felt so bad. Danny told us he was worried about his granddad.

"Why?" we all wanted to know.

"Because he met the King a lot of times during his Navy career, and was decorated by him at Buckingham Palace, he'll be devastated by this."

There was nothing we could say or do about it, except to give Danny as much support as we could. Princess Elizabeth was on all of the newsreels the week following her father's death as she was now Queen of England. Our school, as well as others around the country would now get ready to celebrate the Coronation of the new Monarch, which would take place at Westminster Abbey next year. By then we would all have left this friendly school we had attended for the past five years and gone on to whatever place awaited us after the scholarship exam.

The night before the big raft venture we were back at our hideout planning strategy. At a meeting of adults and organisers of this event both gangs had been told what we could and couldn't do.

"You have decided to turn this into a race," said Commander Phillips. "Alright that's up to you, but please remember you have sponsors, so the further you go the more money you will earn. You'll be able to take reasonable steps to impede your rival's progress, but on no account are you to do anything that will endanger them. I want that clearly understood. If I, or any of the other referees, who will be at different points along the course, see anything they consider dangerous, the offending crew will be stopped straight away and will take no further part. We expect you to use missiles to throw at one another, but here again, nothing that will cause injury. Do I make myself clear?" he barked at all of us.

Both crews solemnly promised to take notice of these warnings and do nothing to cause anyone any harm.

Now Davie was pacing up and down the hideout.

"We have to stop them from getting in front of us at any time, especially before we reach the bend in the river. If they're in front at that point, we'll have to take the outside route and that'll cost us a lot of time."

"We can pelt them with rotten fruit from my dad's shop," Keith Andrews reminded him.

"Yes that'll help but it won't stop them. We've pelted them with all sorts of things before and it only slows them up.

Danny had been silent up till now. "David, are you on the steering oar?"

David Callow was startled to be asked this but replied that yes he would be.

"Then a lot will depend on you. They'll bully us as soon as we start off, by trying to ram us and drive our raft onto the bank. You must see this doesn't happen. As soon as you see them coming towards us you must put us on a collision course with them. Our raft is sturdy enough to withstand this. We'll be pelting them with rotten fruit and veg and that'll be keeping them busy. If we can get over their early tactics we'll have a great chance of not only completing the course, but of beating them into the bargain."

“There speaks the Navy officer,” said Davie. “Ok then, that’s what we’ll do.”

April 24th 1952, and the sun was shining down on the waters of the River Gest. On its surface were two rafts, gently swinging on the mooring ropes that held them securely to a pontoon stretched across the river for this purpose. Lining the banks were spectators from both villages along with interested friends and relatives.

Now, at 10.15 in the morning, both crews stood at their rafts. Convincing ourselves we were so much better than them at anything we did, our raft would have to be much better than theirs. But looking at it now we knew this wasn’t the case. They had put together a craft that was every bit as sturdy as ours. Danny saw the look on my face.

"Don’t worry Billy, we’ll beat them.”

With this we all boarded and waited for the starting flag to drop and the rafts to be released. Ours felt great beneath us and we were very determined she would carry us to victory today. Just as Danny had predicted, we found ourselves under attack as soon as we started off. Brimly’s raft, under the command of Frank Thornton, suddenly veered towards us and their intention was clear. They were trying to ram us and force us into the bank which would have finished our trip right there. But because Danny had foreseen this happening he roared out an order to David Callow, “Turn into them now.”

David swung the big oar we used for steering as far as it would go, and our raft swerved right and met the Brimly’s with a huge bang. We hung on and kept our balance, but they thought they would catch us out with this devious manoeuvre and were not ready for our counter action. When the two crafts hit most of them were thrown off balance and both Bill Grimes and Eddie Compton fell into the water. As they frantically got their wet crew members back on board we were off and away, pelting them with the lovely rotten fruit that Keith Andrews had got for us.

Now with the sail our girls had made for us filling with wind, we were gaining speed and positively rushing along the River Gest. I looked back and saw the Brimly raft, now with everyone back on board, moving after us but a long way behind. We were so happy nothing could stop us now and we knew it, we were cruising and listening to the cheers of our supporters on our side of the river. This kept up all along the route and when we came in sight of Westbridge docks we could hear ships sirens sounding to help us on our way. HMS Dragon came into view and the decks were lined with her crew and our fellow cadets. It was Danny again who saw the danger.

We were so full of ourselves, rushing along the middle of the river with no danger in sight we had stopped looking where we were going. Danny saw Mr Leadbetter frantically waving for us to get further out.

"Trouble everyone," he said.

Looking around we saw at once that we had made the most stupid blunder. The Gest had mud banks at this point and was only deep in the middle. We should have been at our most alert at this time, and tried desperately to correct the damage before it was too late. David Callow swung the oar and we began to turn, but not quickly enough. The raft shuddered under us and came to a complete stop, we had run aground.

"Get your paddles," yelled Danny and when we had complied he had us all pushing them into the mud on the river bank side.

We tried to do what he wanted and get our raft off this mud bank but had no luck at all. We could hear groans, both from the bank and from HMS Dragon, because they could see the Brimly raft out in deep water and coming up fast. As they went past they shouted insults at us as well as making rude signs.

Danny now screamed at us. “Push harder we must get off this mud.”

Responding to the urgency in his voice we pushed our paddles deep into the offending muck and pushed with everything we had. At first nothing happened, but then we felt a shudder as we drifted off the mud and rejoined the river. Our sail filled with wind and we started off in pursuit, but they were now a long way in front and the task before us was daunting.

But we had a very big weapon in our arsenal, in the person of Danny Meadows. He had us all on our knees dipping our paddles in and out of the water in perfect unison, and his voice never stopped urging us on.

“Come on boys use your paddles, dip them in and pull, dip and pull, dip and pull.”

We dipped and pulled with strength we didn’t know we possessed and with Danny’s voice and the cheers of our supporters ringing in our ears we went for glory.

Our bitter rivals raft began to loom larger as we caught up with it. When we reached the back of the Brimly craft Frank Thornton’s voice could be heard. He was now shouting at the top of his voice for his boys to paddle faster.

“One last effort,” shouted Danny. “Come on boys.”

From somewhere we found that last effort he wanted and began to glide alongside the Brimly raft. The finishing line was coming up fast and we were nearly spent, but Danny wouldn’t quit.

"We're there boys, pull. Pull like you've never pulled before."

We did pull, and incredibly, right on the line, the front of our raft went inches past that of the Brimly craft. There was an anxious wait while it was decided that we had in fact come first, then a huge cheer broke out and we were beaming from ear to ear. Commander Phillips was on the bridge carrying the road that led to Westbridge High Street over the river.

Eventually he managed to get silence, then using his loud hailer said, "I think everyone here will agree that these two boy's crews have given us some marvellous entertainment today."

A burst of applause from both sides of the river greeted this statement.

"The boys themselves turned this into a race, and what a close one it turned out to be. They both did what they started out to achieve, and that was to get to this finishing line so really there are no losers here today. Between them they have raised £25.00. Yes," he said as applause burst out from both banks, "they deserve your appreciation. The money they have raised today will go towards the setting up of the Surlington Boys Boxing Club which will be open to all comers. So very well done all of you," he finished.

Frank Thornton then came aboard our raft and walked up to Davie Collins. He braced himself for trouble, but Frank surprised not only him, but all of us as well. He held out his hand to Davie and said, "Well done, your lot did you proud, you deserved to win."

I didn't know it at the time, but this turned out to be an olive branch between our two gangs. Today the rest of the Brimly boys also came aboard and we all shook hands and congratulated each other. Bill Grimes, still soaking wet said, "at least you lot managed to keep dry."

We looked at each other. This was true, we were all bone dry. Not one of us had fallen off the raft. The life preservers we were wearing not having been put to any sort of use. Now the same thought passed through our minds, and with huge grins and a loud shout, all nine of us jumped high in the air and landed with a big splash in the river. When we surfaced I looked towards the bank and saw my dad laughing and my mother with a resigned look on her face that plainly said here we go again. But she smiled at me then turned and started back to our village with dad.

As for the Sundance gang, we spent the rest of the day swimming in the river while our clothes dried out on the bank.

www.ingramcontent.com/pod-product-compliance
Ingram Content Group UK Ltd.
Pitfield, Milton Keynes, MK11 3LW, UK
UKHW020130250726
13967UKWH00002B/565

9 780992 627607